It had been

Alysse might want to pretend that she had some control over her emotions, but she really didn't where Jay was concerned.

He tipped her chin up, looking down at her with those big dark-chocolate-brown eyes of his and he kissed her. His hands framed her face as his mouth moved over hers with the confidence and surety she remembered.

But then he intensified the kiss and she stopped thinking. She just let her feelings take over. Shivers spread down her spine.

She was alive and nothing else mattered to her at this moment.

He swept her off her feet and took a few steps before sitting down on a nearby chair. She straddled him and peered down at him.

"I want you," he said. He took the tip of his finger and drew it down the center of her neck and then caressed the spot above her breasts.

She didn't want to talk. If she did, she'd start thinking and worrying and she'd have to leave.

And right now she was remembering that it had been a very long time since any man had touched her l

ONE MORE KISS

BY
KATHERINE GARBERA

MILLS & BOON

First published in Great Britain 2013
by Mills & Boon, an imprint of Harlequin (UK) Limited,
Eton House, 18-24 Paradise Road, Richmond, Surrey TW9 1SR

© Katherine Garbera 2013

ISBN: 978 0 263 90504 5

30-0313

Harlequin (UK) policy is to use papers that are natural, renewable and recyclable products and made from wood grown in sustainable forests. The logging and manufacturing processes conform to the legal environmental regulations of the country of origin.

Printed and bound in Spain
by Blackprint CPI, Barcelona

Katherine Garbera is a *USA TODAY* bestselling author of more than forty books who has always believed in happy endings. She lives in England with her husband, children and their pampered pet, Godiva. Visit Katherine on the web at www.katherinegarbera.com, or catch up with her on Facebook and Twitter.

I have to thank Julie Leto who was very helpful when I asked for her advice on writing for Blaze. She gave me her insights, which as always were spot-on. Also thanks to Brenda Chin and Kathryn Lye for liking my idea when I sent it to them!

This book is dedicated to my sister Linda and her family, James, Katie and Ryan, who made us so happy to call Southern California home and who shared their friends with us and they became our friends, as well. So a shout-out to Brit, Amy and Jason, who made us feel welcome.

1

"MARRY ME," Gunnery Sergeant Mac said as he took the small box filled with four of her signature chocolate "sin" cupcakes. They were her number-one seller in the bakeshop, Sweet Dreams.

"I can't, Mac, you only love me for my cupcakes," Alysse Dresden replied. The uniformed Marine came in here once a week and every time asked her the same mock question.

"We can work around that, I can come to love you for your other assets," he said as he headed toward the door.

Alysse laughed as the soldier left and she turned to her next customer. Sweet Dreams was the culmination of four years of hard work. She got at least two marriage proposals a day at her bakery and usually a few professions of undying love. Her mother hadn't been wrong when she said the way to a man's heart was through his stomach.

If only her mother had told her how to keep a man once she got his attention with food. Alas, she hadn't, and Alysse had one failed marriage behind her. But that disaster wasn't one that should be dwelt on.

"You should take him up on his offer," Staci Rowland said as she came in from the back with a tray of red velvet cupcakes.

"Mac?" Alysse asked. She wasn't about to marry a man she barely knew. She'd been there, done that and had burned the T-shirt.

"Yes, or any of the other guys who come through here," Staci said as she placed the tray in the display counter.

Staci was her business partner and the cocreator of Sweet Dreams. They'd met almost four years ago in a local baking competition. They'd competed with each other for a few years trying to outsell and out-create each other around town before they'd decided to work together and open the bakery. The rest, as they say, was history.

"They aren't serious. They just like my cakes," Alysse said, knowing what she said was true. Though she wished sometimes that some of the men were at least interested in a few casual dates, they never were.

"Of course they do, but unless you go out with one of them you're never going to find the one guy who wants more than baked goods from you," Staci said.

Staci was five foot four and had short black hair that she wore in a pixie cut. She was petite but had more curves than Alysse, who was tall with a more athletic build. Where Alysse overanalyzed every action before she took it, Staci tended to jump and then hope a net would appear. They were opposites in everything except their desire to make Sweet Dreams a success.

"That guy was pretty hot, you should have—"

"Ugh!" Alysse said to Staci. "Besides, hot doesn't mean he's the right guy for me."

She was living proof of that. Damn. Why was she dwelling on her ex today? She wanted to pretend she didn't really know, but this week…it was the four-year anniversary of her waking up alone in the honeymoon suite of the Golden Dream Hotel in Vegas.

"It doesn't mean he's the *wrong* guy for you, either," Staci chastised. "You have a thing against men in uniform. Why?"

"They're cocky and they really can't commit to a woman. And for the record, it's not like I don't go on dates," Alysse said. She'd never talked about her brief marriage.

"You've given the usual dating websites a try and I'll admit they aren't exactly gleaming with amazing guys, but I think you don't want to find a man."

"Do you?" Alysse asked. To be honest, there were times when she was lonely, but the risk of falling for the wrong guy was too high for her to take the chance. She didn't ever again want to feel the way she had when Jay had walked away. *Ever.*

"No, but I at least enjoy being single," Staci said. "Going out to clubs. And you don't."

"I'm sorry I couldn't go with you last night. I had already promised my brother that I'd hang out with him."

"Well, I'm surprised you went since it was just your brother and about fifteen hot guys."

Alysse shook her head. "Toby's friends are my friends. We grew up surfing together and playing beach volleyball. Going out with them…it's fun."

"It's safe," Staci said. "There's no risk for you. Why do you do that?"

Alysse shrugged. It was safe going out with them because Toby's friends treated her like their little sister. And when she was out on the waves, surfing with them they treated her like an anonymous person—just another surfer.

"Most people don't want to risk their hearts," Alysse answered.

Staci came over and gave her a hug. From the beginning, Staci's caring heart had surprised Alysse, because her friend looked tough. Her hair was cut in a trendy fashion but she presented herself to the world as if she were a badass.

"Honey, safe isn't doing it for you. Something is missing in your life. I just want you to be happy," Staci said.

"Me, too." Alysse really craved happiness but had no idea how to get it. She'd thought that the bakery was the solution but the longer they worked at it and the more success and accolades she achieved at Sweet Dreams, the bigger that longing inside of her grew.

The phone rang before Staci could respond and Alysse reached around her to answer it. The phone was an old-fashioned wall-mounted unit that had come with the bakery when they'd bought the property.

"Sweet Dreams Bakery, home of the incredible red velvet dream cupcakes."

"Hello," the caller said. His voice was deep and raspy, vaguely familiar, but then she talked to men on the phone all the time.

Staci just mouthed over to her that the discussion

wasn't over and went to help a customer who had entered the shop. Alysse leaned back against the wall and twirled the phone cord around her finger.

"What can I do for you today?" she asked.

"I have a dessert emergency," he said.

"An emergency? Well, we will be happy to help you out," she said. She liked creating desserts that were unique to the person who would eat them. It wasn't always easy to do, but she'd done it more than once with a lot of success. In fact, she'd been featured in a regional magazine after she'd made an anniversary cake for the deputy mayor of San Diego.

"I was hoping you'd say that," he said.

His voice was perfect, she thought. She closed her eyes and just let the sound of it wash over her. This was what was wrong with her, she thought, snapping her eyes open and staring at the photo of cupcakes mounted on the wall behind the phone. She was afraid of a man who walked into her bakery but one she could flirt with on the phone, one who was safely isolated, she could handle.

"What can I get for you?" she asked. She pulled a prestamped notepad closer and got ready to jot down the details. She and Staci had made these forms up after they'd botched an order writing it down on napkins. That had been a long time ago, but they still wrote everything down on the notepad.

"I need something…different. I made some mistakes where my lady is concerned and I want to make it up to her," he said, his voice low yet sincere.

Alysse knew she was a softy when it came to men making big romantic gestures. One time she'd stayed up all night making an anniversary cake for a man who'd forgotten to order it in advance and needed it first thing in the morning. She'd charged him double to justify staying overnight to bake it, but in her heart she liked that he'd realized he'd screwed up and tried to make up for it.

"Then this is going to have to be a really special cupcake or maybe a cookie. Tell me about her," Alysse invited.

Sweet Dreams had cultivated a reputation in San Diego of being the place for one-of-a-kind desserts, mainly because she and Staci both believed that making something special was more than worth their time. People would pay for good food and that was what they delivered.

"Hmm…that's not easy. She's kind of elusive and hard to figure out."

It was always interesting to her the way men described the women they loved. She and Staci had an annual Valentine's Day contest where couples competed to come up with the perfect treat for each other by describing what the other person was like. The winners were chosen from those who described their mate and picked the perfect dessert.

"That's probably why you like her," Alysse said. "Men like a mystery."

He sighed and she thought she heard a honking horn behind him. "That we do. But I'm used to solving them."

She jotted down *mysterious* on the order form. Every guy thought women were hard to figure out, but if they just paid attention, she thought, it would be mystery solved. She'd never known a woman yet who didn't in her own way tell a man exactly what she wanted.

"What else can you tell me about her?" Alysse asked.

"She's feisty and spicy in bed," he said. "She knows how to both satisfy a man and leave him wanting more."

She made a few more notes and then put her pen down. Well, it sounded as though he had found him a woman who met all of Alysse's own perceptions of what the male fantasy was.

"Is she sweet?" Alysse asked.

"Semisweet," he said. "She's got a kind of gentleness to her that is at odds with that fiery temper of hers."

She turned to look at the stainless-steel counters of the kitchen area of the bakery.

"Okay, I think I've got it. Do you want a small cake or a cupcake?" she asked. She already had an idea in mind for the batter—a kind of a riff on her Redemption Cake. She made it often enough out of a basic chocolate cake recipe and added special ingredients to make it personal to the couple.

"Surprise me," he said.

"I will. When do you need it?" she asked. She figured she'd work on the recipe overnight and try a couple of variations so that she got the perfect recipe for this guy. She was going to be charging him a high price for this unique cake and she wanted to ensure he got his money's worth.

"This evening."

"Uh…I'm not sure I can do that. We close at six,"

she said. She could also spend the afternoon in the kitchen working on this special order instead of helping customers and listening to Staci tell her she didn't date the right guys, which—she wasn't going to lie—sounded ideal. But this guy was asking for the moon.

"Perfect. I'll pay you to deliver it to the Hotel Del Coronado—the Beach Villas."

"Um…we don't usually do that."

"Please," he said, his sexy voice dropping a bit to become even deeper. "I won't ask again."

A shiver spread down her arms and across her chest. There was something familiar about that low tone but then she always associated sexy with Jay Michener, her ex-husband. And Jay was the last man who'd be pulling out all the stops to win back a woman. That wasn't his style. No. Walking away without looking back was his style, and she needed to remember that.

"I think you might be my only chance," he said.

Alysse shook her head at her own weakness for romance. What was her deal?

"Okay. I'll do it," she said. "Should I leave it at the desk?"

"No, I'm having a dinner catered for us on the beach. Can you bring it down there?"

She should say no, but this man who was going to such lengths to win back his lady intrigued her. "I'll do it. What's your name?"

"Just ask for the Marine," he said.

"Okay. I'll need your credit-card information," she said. She wasn't about to do all that work without being paid.

"I'll pay when you get here."

He hung up before she could get any more details. She turned around to see that the shop was empty again and Staci was watching her.

"Order?" she asked.

"A mystery order from a sexy-voiced guy," Alysse said, trying to sound light. But this Marine and his order was affecting her and making her think of things that she usually kept tucked away. She decided to trust that he could pay her; he was staying at the Coronado and it wasn't exactly cheap.

"Tell me more."

She shrugged. How could she describe what he wanted her to do without letting Staci know that her hard heart was melting? "He wants something special to try to win back his girl."

"What are you going to make?" Staci asked, focusing on the food like a good baker.

"I don't know. I was going to go and pull ingredients that fit his description of her." She liked this part of the process. Baking was as easy to her as breathing. She knew the recipes and then just changed up the ingredients until she had something unique.

"And that would be?" Staci asked. "Let me guess, sexy?"

Alysse laughed because so many guys said that when they were asked about their women. But once the probing went a little deeper the answers started to vary.

"More specifically, spicy, unpredictable and semisweet," she said.

"Sounds like a challenge. When do you need it?" Staci asked, wiping down the counter.

"Tonight. I told him I'd deliver it to the Hotel Del Coronado."

"Why are you delivering it?" Staci asked. "Girl, be serious here. We don't do this kind of thing."

"He had a really sexy voice and he said please," Alysse said. It sounded lame as a reason even to her.

"He's taken," Staci said, shaking her head as she walked across the room. "He wants a dessert for his lady."

"I know. I just… It's romantic, isn't it? That he'd go to that much trouble to get her back," Alysse said.

"He must have really made a mess of their relationship," Staci, ever the realist, said.

Big-time, Alysse agreed. But that didn't change the fact that he was trying to make up for it. That earned him major points in her book.

"Probably. Would you take a guy back if he planned a dinner for you at the Coronado on the beach?" Alysse asked her friend.

"Not sure. I guess it would depend on the guy," she said with a shrug. "I'm not much on forgiving."

"Me, neither," Alysse said.

Maybe that was why she had said yes to delivering the dessert. She wanted this couple to have a second chance at love. A second chance at making their relationship work—because her own lover had never even tried for a second chance.

Even if he had she would have said no, she thought. She left the store area and went back into the kitchen. It was time for her to do the one thing that she was genuinely good at—taking ingredients and mixing them into something edible, something mouthwatering and delicious. It wasn't lost on her that she used her baking to escape from the real world. In here she was in charge and if anything went wrong she could toss it out and start over.

She weighed and measured the cocoa and the flour and sifted them together, taking a kind of comfort from the mixing. She tried to keep the image of Jay from her mind but she couldn't. The memory of the tough-as-Pittsburgh-steel Marine Corps sniper was hard to ignore. She knew that was why she'd failed at blind dates and speed-dating. She measured every man she met by the yardstick that was Jay, or by what she'd thought Jay was when she'd married him, and no one, not even Jay, would ever measure up.

JAY MICHENER TOOK a swallow of his beer and leaned back against the wall behind him. The bar was more open than he felt comfortable in; since he'd gotten back from Afghanistan he couldn't relax. There were three other guys at the table with him.

Lucien he knew well as they'd been in the same unit for two tours. They'd been to the Middle East and back several times. Lucien had gotten out of the Corps two years ago and had started his own security business with the other two men at the table.

Jay didn't know either man well, but they felt like guys he'd known before. But then, Jay had spent all of his adult life in the military so there weren't many enlisted men he couldn't relate to. The two men got up to play pool and Lucien took a sip of his beer before turning to Jay.

"Why don't you come by my office tomorrow and

I'll give you the tour? Show you what life is like on the outside," Lucien said with a wry grin.

"The outside? It's not like I've been in prison," Jay said. The Corps was his life not because he had no other choices but because it was where he wanted to be.

"It sort of is. You've been in since you were eighteen and you're pushing thirty now. Isn't it time you tried something else?" Lucien asked.

"Maybe," Jay said. "I'll try to swing by tomorrow."

"Don't 'try to,' be there around ten, Lance Corporal," Lucien said.

"Okay," Jay told him, giving in. It couldn't hurt to check out Lucien's place.

"You free for dinner?" Lucien asked.

"Why?"

"I want you to meet my girlfriend," Lucien said. "She's always bugging me to bring home the guys I talk about."

"I can't tonight," Jay said. *Or ever,* he thought. He couldn't think of anything more torturous than spending the night with Lucien and his girlfriend talking about the old times.

"I've gotta go," Jay said, glancing at his watch. He wasn't a guy who normally took gambles, so this one with Alysse was odd. But she had always made him feel differently than other women did, which was probably why he'd married her four years ago. That was probably also the chief reason he'd left her after only one week.

He was dressed casually in a pair of faded jeans and a T-shirt but he felt naked without his rifle in his hand. How was a man supposed to live when he was always on edge? With Alysse, he had hoped to find something more normal, but the week they'd spent together had made him realize that he felt even more vulnerable with her.

Now he was stationed at Pendleton in Oceanside, California, about a twenty-minute drive north of San Diego. Pendleton had an idyllic setting right across the 5 from the Pacific Ocean and it was easy sometimes to forget that there was anything else but the beach and an endless horizon.

But his mind hadn't let Alysse go as easily as Jay had hoped. Every night she sneaked into his dreams— and the sexy ones weren't the problem. It was the normal-life ones that really disturbed Jay. The ones where he pictured Alysse in an apron with a few kids at her feet were the worst because he didn't believe he was ever going to be the man who gave her those things.

"You're on leave, Lance Corporal, I didn't think you had anywhere to be," Lucien said.

"I do tonight."

There was a lot of laughing at the table as the men all made some comment about women and hot dates. He smiled and let them think it was just a casual hookup. He waved goodbye and walked out of the bar in San Diego's Gaslamp district.

He got on his Ducati 1100s motorcycle and drove to the Hotel Del Coronado. He didn't make a lot of money as a sniper in the U.S. Marine Corps but Jay didn't spend a lot of money either. He didn't have an apartment or house of his own, preferring to stay in hotels when he was on leave. Since he had always planned to be a career military man, he used base housing and stored his Ducati when he was deployed.

But something had changed in him on this last deployment. He had no idea if it was the fact that he'd turned thirty or the fact that he was at a crossroads. He could get out of the Corps now, find a civilian job and maybe have a shot at normality. Though he wasn't convinced he was cut out for normal.

Tricking Alysse wasn't the answer, but the last time he'd had a shot at a real life had been with her. His commanding officer would say he was being a, well… a coward, for lack of a better word, and Jay knew the CO would be right. But he wanted Alysse back.

His plan—and he always had a plan—was to spend his leave here with Alysse Dresden and figure out if he was meant for this life or if he should stay being a warrior.

Still, he needed to make up for how he'd left her. He hoped the romantic setting and the surprise of the grand gesture would be enough of an olive branch to persuade her to give him a second chance.

He pulled his bike to a stop in front of the villa he was renting and went inside and showered and changed. He'd spent a lot of time thinking up this strategy. He knew better than just to call and ask Alysse out. He'd hurt her and he knew it. The fact that he'd thought of nothing but her for the last four years had sent a strong message to him that he needed some kind of closure with her.

He took his time setting up the area, just as he would to get ready for a target. Planning and execution were the keys to success and he never forgot that. The staff had laid out a bamboo rug and then set the table up on that. Twinkle lights hung from the ceiling of the cabana. There were curtains which had been drawn back to let the breeze flow through the structure.

Jay was a little wary of having so much open space around him, but he was on leave and he tried not to let it bother him. He hated how on edge he always was when he came in from the field. And tonight he was doubly edgy because of Alysse.

He scanned the beach and the area where he was standing looking for the best strategic advantage. He sat at the table but felt stupid just sitting there, so he got up. He checked the wine chilling in the freestanding ice bucket and then walked to the edge of the cabana to lean against a palm tree.

Just as he decided he looked like someone in an all-inclusive resort commercial, Alysse appeared. He realized all at once he wasn't as prepared as he'd hoped to be, because he'd forgotten how beautiful she was.

She arrived just as the sun was starting to set. She wore a casual skirt, and a blousy shirt. But it wasn't the clothes—more the body underneath it. She was tall—almost five-foot-seven—and had an athletic build. She moved with grace and confidence and he couldn't tear his eyes from her.

He had his sunglasses on. Her long ginger hair blew in the wind, a tendril brushing over her cheek and her lips. She moved with fluid grace and ease. She stopped on the path and glanced at the cabana. Was she wary of coming out here on her own?

"Hello? Marine?" Alysse called out.

Jay stayed where he was, watching her, feeling a little like a voyeur, but this was probably the only chance he'd have to observe her before she recognized him. He could turn around and walk away from this beach and this woman, just walk back to his Ducati and get the hell out of here.

"Hello?"

There was a catch in her voice and he knew he couldn't just leave. He didn't want to. There was a reason he was here and the reason had everything to do with this woman.

"Hello, Alysse," he said, stepping from the shadows.

She shook her head and then pushed her sunglasses up, revealing her narrowed eyes. She took two angry steps toward him.

"Jay?" she asked. "Is that really you?"

He took a step closer to her. He was so close he could smell the homey scent of vanilla and see the freckles that dotted her cheekbones.

"Yes."

She threw the cake box on the table and clenched her hands. "You ass."

"I guess I deserve that," he said.

She shook her head. "You deserve a lot more than that."

"Yes, ma'am."

"I never thought I'd see you again," she said, more to herself. She took a step back from him and then pivoted and he realized she was leaving.

"Wait."

"Why should I?" she asked.

He took two steps toward her and reached out to touch her but she flinched away.

"I…I'm sorry for the way I left," he said.

She nodded, but he couldn't tell what she was thinking. "I had to get back to base. The way we met and married I never had a chance to tell you I only had a week of leave."

"You couldn't wake me up to tell me or maybe leave me a note?" she asked.

Of course he could have, but Alysse had made him think about something other than getting laid, and no woman had done that before. "I didn't mean to marry you."

"I know that. It was Vegas that made us both act the way we did," she said. "Here's your dessert. I guess your technique with women hasn't improved if you needed something special to win her back."

"It's for you," he said.

"It's going to take a hell of a lot more than a cupcake to win me back."

"I know. Stay for dinner tonight."

She shook her head. "Give me one good reason. Why should I stay with the man who abandoned me?"

"We have unfinished business, Aly, you know it and I know it. That's why I left the way I did."

"I've moved on."

He knew she meant it to hurt him and it did. But he'd already recognized that this was going to be one of the toughest missions he'd ever been on and he didn't mind working to get Alysse back.

2

ALYSSE DIDN'T THINK as highly of Jay's idea now that she realized she was the woman in question. There wasn't any dessert in the world that would make a woman forgive being left on the last day of her honeymoon by her husband. Especially not if the woman in question was her. A cake couldn't fix the way he'd abandoned her.

Last night she'd had a good time hanging out with her brother and his friends, who were all extreme athletes. Two of them were pro surfers, another two pro skateboarders and Toby was a semi-pro beach volleyball player. She understood that men could let something other than a woman dominate their lives—for Jay it was service to his country. But all of the men she knew had learned how to balance their careers with a relationship. Something that Jay seemed not to have done.

A part of her still wanted him, though. He was dressed in a skintight black T-shirt that showed off his muscles, he was cleanly shaven and she noticed a new scar along the left side of his jaw. How had he gotten that?

He was a Marine who had been in a combat zone; she knew that from trying to track him down to get their divorce finalized. He held himself tensely. His eyes were narrowed and, though he kept his attention on her, she knew he was aware of their surroundings.

"Why are you looking at me?" he asked as he held the chair out for her to sit down. "Do you want to curse at me again?"

She felt a little embarrassed at what she'd done but mostly she felt justified. It was better than her other impulse which had been to start screaming at him. Or worse, to start crying. She doubted that he'd believe how deeply he'd hurt her. After all, as her mom had pointed out, they'd only known each other for a week. But that week had changed her life.

"Maybe," she said. But she knew she wouldn't do it. She wanted answers from him. And if she got nothing else out of this dinner, she promised herself at least she'd leave with a better understanding of why she'd been attracted to him and why even a divorce didn't seem final enough for her to forget him.

He set the bakery box on the table between them. She looked at the bottle of wine chilling in the ice bucket and realized he'd remembered what she drank— Santa Margherita pinot grigio. *Good for him,* she thought, trying not to let it matter.

"I really am sorry about the way I left," he said. "It was a cowardly thing to do."

"I'd have thought your Marine code would have a rule about that."

"Not a rule exactly," he said wryly.

She didn't want to flirt with him and talk about the

Corps. That easy charm was part of what had attracted her to him in the first place, but she knew now that there was nothing easy about Jay Michener.

"Why did you do it?" she asked. She couldn't figure out why he'd asked her to marry him. She'd accepted because it had fitted into her plans. She'd just finished cooking school and the next thing on her to-do list was to start a family. She'd always wanted one and when she'd met Jay in Vegas it had seemed as if fate had stepped in.

"I don't know," he said.

"Honestly? You must have some clue," she said. She wasn't going to let him get away with lying to her. *Not now.* He'd broken her heart. That wasn't right.

"No. That's not true. I left because you tempted me to stay," he said. "And I had a job to do. And in the end the job won."

Brutal.

But what else had she expected? That was another little nugget for her to tuck away and make sure she never let this man's charm win her over again.

"Why am I here now? Are you on leave again and thought we could hook up?" she asked.

"Yes, I'm on leave, and as you pointed out I owe you some explanations."

She leaned back in her chair and took in the scene. The table had been set up with a pretty white damask tablecloth. With the setting sun and private beach, he'd gotten the romance of this moment perfect. But she no longer believed that Jay was the right man for this kind of special moment.

"I'm not sure I'm following you—you came back to explain?"

"No. I came back to see if you would listen to me. Maybe give me a second chance."

"At what?"

He arched one eyebrow at her. "At us."

She shook her head. "You want to get married again?"

He shrugged. And her heart fell. He wasn't here for her. He was here to bring closure to his past. And if she was honest with herself, she'd already let Jay use her enough for this lifetime.

"No thanks."

She honestly believed that Jay was a warrior. A man more at home with his unit on a mission. Having been a soldier his entire adult life he had no idea how to share himself with others.

"I asked around, you're still single."

"I own my own business, which takes up a lot of my time," she said, not sure how she felt about him asking about her.

"Granted."

"What do you want me to say, Jay?"

"That you'll give us a second chance."

"But you're making no promises? I'm not an idiot," she said.

"I know that. Neither am I. And I'll tell you this, I've never been able to forget you, Aly. There's not a day that goes by that I don't think about you. I know I hurt you and don't really deserve a second chance, but I'm asking you to give me one."

He was sincere; she could read that easily enough

in his eyes. But she didn't want to trust him again. For some reason she'd fallen for him—the quiet loner with the easy charm instead of the outgoing athletic guys she usually hung out with.

"I'm sorry. But I don't think I should be here. You enjoy the dessert and have a great life, Jay."

She grabbed her purse and started to walk away and he followed her again, this time when he grabbed her arm he wouldn't let her shake him off.

"No, don't leave. I'm sorry. I'm not handling this right, but I don't know what else to do. I need to figure out things that have nothing to do with the Corps."

"I don't see how that affects me," she said. She tried not to let it bother her that he thought about her.

"I guess I want you to give me a second chance, not to leave you again but to love you."

"I don't think I can do that, Jay," she said. "You broke my heart and didn't have the guts to stay and tell me you were leaving."

"I can't tell you how sorry I am for that," he said. "But I can show you that I've changed."

"Have you?" she asked. Because so far she wasn't seeing any big differences.

He started to nod, but then stopped. "I hope so. But I really don't know. I've been on back-to-back deployments so I haven't had a chance even to breathe since the last time I saw you."

She tugged her arm from his grip and stood staring at him in the fading light. She could use some closure herself. Maybe then she'd be able to really move on from Jay.

For too long he'd been the reason she'd stayed sin-

gle, afraid to risk herself again. He'd changed her from
the girl who'd always said yes to life to someone who'd
started living in the shadows. That was it, she thought
as she stood staring at him in the fading twilight.

She'd given him her heart after a whirlwind courtship and gotten burned and now...now she wanted a
chance to reclaim her heart and her faith in men. Because her short marriage was the reason why she was
too afraid to let anyone in.

Maybe this would heal her.

"If I give you this chance, it might not work out for
you," she said. "I'm not sure I can ever trust you again."

"I understand. It's my mission to make you trust
me," he said.

She had to think this through. On the surface it
seemed the perfect way for her to get on with her life.
She had poured her heart and soul into Sweet Dreams
and now the bakery was doing better than she or Staci
had ever hoped it would. But what was next? They had
been talking about opening a second location, but that
was more work. She used work as the excuse to her
family and friends as the reason why she didn't date.
Now Jay was back and until she resolved her past with
him she'd never be able to move on. He was offering
her a lot more than he probably realized.

"There was something powerful between us or we
wouldn't have been attracted to each other the first
time."

"We can try to get to know each other again, Jay,
but I'm going to use this time to get over you."

Jay crossed his big-muscled arms over his chest. It
would help her to get over him if he'd let himself go

physically in the four years since she'd last seen him. But no, he was still in top form. His thick brown hair was still military short and his eyes had a few more sun lines around them than he had before.

And he looked older, but not in a bad way. He had more experience and he wore it with an ease that she hoped she did, as well. She still wanted him. She had wished she wouldn't.

The thought of those big arms wrapping around her and holding her made her close her eyes. She remembered the way his legs had tangled with hers and how they'd fitted together perfectly.

"Fair enough," he said, holding up his hands. "If I can't convince myself we deserve a second chance then how the hell am I going to convince you?"

He was asking her to trust him, though he didn't recognize it. She had to believe she was strong enough to protect her heart this time. She had to believe that she was strong enough to resist the lust and emotions he drew effortlessly from her.

And yet, she wanted him. It had been four long years since she'd been in the same space as this man. She'd never admit it out loud, but she had sort of feared he'd die on deployment and she'd never know. That she'd spend the rest of her life wondering what had happened to him.

And though she still wasn't sure this was the wisest course of action, she found that that one thing hadn't changed in four years.

It was her intent that this time she'd walk away the winner. She was intrigued enough by Jay to want to stay, and having a plan made her feel that much better about it. But the truth was he was her fatal weakness and something she was determined to change.

JAY KNEW HOW FRAGILE his control over Alysse was. He had thought an apology would be enough at least to get them back to a nice place to start over. But now he was admitting that wouldn't do it. How out of touch he was struck him.

How could he convince her to trust him when he wasn't too sure that leaving the Corps and starting over was what he truly wanted? He should have dinner with her and then send her on her way. She deserved a new start without him possibly dragging her down.

And that was the rub. In the field he was confident of his abilities. All the training and missions he'd had ensured that when he took aim he hit his target. But alone on the beach with Alysse, now that was something he wasn't as confident of.

"Will you come back and have a glass of wine with me?" he asked.

"Yes," she said. "But I don't think I should stay for dinner."

He escorted Alysse back to the table and for the first time understood how hard this mission was going to be. He wanted a second chance to make things right with her. He'd never meant for her to get hurt the way she had.

He poured them each a glass of wine. Their two-day affair had led to marriage and one week of red-hot sex in the honeymoon suite. He still couldn't believe that he'd married her. When he'd been with her, he'd felt young—though he was only a year older than her.

He'd always felt older, but not during that week. He'd felt young and a little bit carefree. That had all changed on the last night.

But he didn't want to think about that now. Instead he looked at the way her pretty red hair blew around her shoulders. That attraction hadn't dulled at all. She was dressed casually and had clearly been working all day but she was still the most beautiful woman in the world to him.

"Tell me about your job. Are you a baker or what at Sweet Dreams?" he asked. He'd found her the old-fashioned way. Followed his lawyer's address that she'd used to send him the divorce papers. He'd been surprised she'd used a business address but really shouldn't have been. She'd been very clear in her letter to him that every conversation between them go through their lawyers.

"I own the bakery with a partner. We've been open almost three years," she said as she took a sip of her wine. There was a faint smile on her face and she traced the raised lettering on the dessert box she'd brought.

"From what I hear on base and around town, you're very successful."

He'd asked about the bakery and had heard tales of the sexy redhead who worked behind the counter. He'd been jealous of the admiration that the other men had for her. She was his, but he knew he'd given up any claims to her when he'd walked away. And that hadn't sat well with him.

"We are," she said. "But then we put everything we have into it. Staci and I have to be at the shop every morning by four to start baking. Usually we try to have a seasonal cupcake so we brainstorm ideas for our next one and then once a week do a sample in the store to judge its success."

"That makes for a very long day." She would have to be pretty tired come evening.

"But I love what I do," she said, then flushed.

There was passion in her voice and something that sounded like joy. She'd found her calling and clearly loved her life. But it seemed as one-sided as his was. "It really gave me something to focus on."

"I'm sorry for the way I left you. Why did you marry me?" he asked. "I've always wondered. You didn't seem like the kind of woman to fall so quickly."

She shrugged and looked away. "You know. I was excited about finishing cooking school and celebrating in Vegas."

"Vegas was a riot, wasn't it?" he asked.

"Definitely. I guess I forgot that it wasn't real, you know. The lights and the people, and you were so good with the grand gestures. I don't even remember you asking me to marry you but I do remember standing in that chapel."

"Me, too."

"Why did you marry me?"

"You made me feel like I was a part of the world and not just an observer," he said.

He'd known from a very early age that he was bound for the military. He'd always had an affinity for weapons and had gone hunting with his dad and uncles from the time he was eight. A certain sense had enabled him to sight his target and make his shot.

"I know you're in the Marines, Jay, but I know so little else about you."

She pushed a strand of hair behind her ear and tipped her head to the side to study him. He wondered what she saw when she looked at him. He knew he was in top physical form thanks to the rigorous requirements of the Corps, but beyond that what did she see?

"I'm a sniper. And have been just about my entire career."

He didn't talk about his work and wouldn't do it now except to give an overview of what he did. This was one part of his life that he never wanted Alysse to be too familiar with.

"Oh. And you like it?" she asked.

"I guess," he said. He wasn't about to reveal his near miss in Afghanistan or how it had hit him hard that he might die and no one would even care. That changed a man, but not in a way he wanted anyone else to know. Especially a woman he was hoping to woo back into his arms. It had made him return to the past and acknowledge he needed to make amends for how he'd left her.

"I don't know, Jay. If you want me to trust you, you have to open up a little more than that," she said.

"You're not going to make this easy, are you?" he asked.

She shook her head. "Nope. I know that it's not very nice but we did easy the first time and look how that turned out."

He doubted that she didn't really care. He'd hurt her and he wouldn't blame her if she wanted to wound him the same way. He deserved that for running out on his marriage to her.

He was relieved when he heard the sound of footsteps behind them and glanced over to see the waiter from the hotel delivering their salads. Food was the distraction they needed so he didn't have to continue to answer uncomfortable questions about himself.

He wasn't sure that this plan of his was being executed to its best advantage. He needed to regroup. But he didn't want just to approach Alysse as though she was a mission. He kept getting distracted by the scent of her perfume and the way her hair blew in the wind.

After the waiter left, he lifted his glass toward her. "To second chances."

"To *earned* second chances," she said, taking a sip of her wine. "I'm sorry if I sounded mean before…"

He had to laugh. It was not Alysse's nature to speak harshly to anyone. He'd learned that during their week together. "You didn't. Don't apologize for your anger at me. I feel incredibly lucky that you agreed to stay for dinner."

"I'm not sure I agreed, but I do have a lot of questions about the way our marriage ended and about you," she said.

"You deserve to have them answered and much more. But not tonight," he said.

She gave him a hard-level stare and he knew she was searching for answers in his eyes. He didn't know what the future held so he tried to convey the only thing he was certain of, which was his sincerity.

They ate dinner and talked about things that didn't really matter to him. Books and movies that he hadn't seen or read; he was behind on his popular culture. And there was a little awkwardness to the evening. But that was to be expected. What he hadn't anticipated was how much he wanted her still. And that that was the only thing he could think about.

"How long are you on leave?" Alysse asked after the waiters had left.

"Two weeks. I'm actually due to sign my reenlistment papers soon," he said.

"And what?" she asked. "You want to spend them with me?"

"I'd like to."

"I'm not changing my life for you, Jay."

"I don't expect you to," he said. "I know that I'm very lucky that you agreed to have dinner with me."

She gave him a half smile. "You *are* lucky. Are you thinking about getting out of the Corps?" she asked.

"I really don't know. When we're done eating I'll take you on a ride on my Ducati, so you can let the wind clear your mind."

"Um…a ride on a motorcycle will likely make me feel like I'm going to die," she said.

"Ah, I won't drive like a maniac, you'll be safe with me. I promise."

She didn't want to believe him, but she did. She wanted to hold on to her anger and just stew in it for as long as she could, because being angry was insulation against starting to feel again.

"I'll think about it. If you don't go back in the Corps what will you do?" she asked.

"A lot of that depends on you."

"It can't. You have to want to get out for yourself."

"I don't really know," he said, then pushed his hands

through his hair. "I hate being indecisive but my future isn't as set in stone as it once was."

"Why?" she asked. "Did something happen? Our marriage wasn't enough to change your mind?"

"Nothing happened," he said. Nothing he wanted to talk about at least, she thought. He'd been raised to be strong and he wasn't going to admit to her that he was a little scared of the future. "I'm just getting older," he told her.

She knew there was more to it than that but he was still not ready to really talk to her. She put her napkin on her plate and stood up.

"It's been nice but I think I'll be going," she said.

"Why? What did I say?"

"It's what you're not saying. You ask me to give you a second chance. Telling me nice-sounding platitudes and then when I ask you for something real, it's back to the smoke and mirrors."

She stared down at him. And then, when he kept silent, she shook her head. "Good luck, Jay."

"Wait. Let's go for a walk… I'll tell you what's going on," he said.

"Okay, but you asked me to trust you, and I'm not sure I can but I'm at least trying. I need to know that you're doing the same," she said.

"I'll try, I'm not any good at this sort of thing, which is why I probably should have just stayed out of your life."

"If you believe that, why are you back here?" she asked. "Why did you call Sweet Dreams and order dessert for a woman—me—to try to win her back?"

"I want something more," he said. "I had a close call

on my last deployment and I realized that I really don't want to live the rest of my life alone—without you."

She didn't either, which was why she'd always been…waiting for the right guy.

For honesty, that was pretty much on the mark. And his words made her admit that she didn't want him to be alone, but that didn't mean that she wanted to be the woman at his side. Jay was difficult to get to know and it was only tonight that she was coming to understand how difficult. That week together had been almost a fairy tale and she'd seen in Jay only what she'd wanted to. A man who was enamored with her and as caught up in the whirlwind romance as she had been.

"What do you want?" she asked.

"I have two weeks to figure it out," he said. "I'm having lunch with some buddies who got out last year," Jay said. "Something might come of that. If I can't find work do you think you could use another cake-froster?"

"Cake-frosting is a delicate art. It requires a skill set you might not have." He'd given her a little nugget of truth and then turned the topic to something safer and she let him do it. She wasn't sure how much "truth" she could take tonight. Seeing him was enough of a shock, learning that he'd almost died before he could come back to her… Well, that was something she didn't want to dwell on.

"What skills exactly?" he asked. "I have steady hands."

He held his big hands out to her. They were tanned and had blunt-trimmed nails. They were the hands of a man who took care of himself. No metrosexual manicure, but looked after all the same.

"That's only part of it. I'd have to see how good you are using them," she said, flirting just a little because she wanted him. And to be honest, flirting was safe. She flirted with uniformed Marines every day and nothing came of it.

"I thought that would be the one thing you'd know I could do," he said.

She shivered as she remembered his hands on her body. He was very good at using them. He was a thorough lover who had taken his time with her, every time. The attention he'd lavished on her had made her feel like the most fascinating woman in the world.

"That's a different type of hand work," she said.

"Really?" he asked in a teasing smile.

"I didn't mean it that way!"

"Of course you didn't," he said with a laugh. It sounded rusty.

"You'd be bored," she said. "It's quiet and repetitive. Most of the stuff we do for decoration is simple flowers or candies. Staci and I do all the work ourselves because it's our favorite part of the job."

"I get your passion. You both have a stake in making sure the business is successful, I'm sure it shows in your work," he said.

"Yes, it does. You'll be able to tell when we have dessert," she said.

"What did you make for my mystery woman?" he asked.

"Wait and see."

"About working at the bakery, I don't think I'd get bored. Plus, you'd be there…we'd have some frosting."

"Okay, enough with that. This is a first date not—"

"Not what? Our last first date ended pretty well."

"The date did, but what happened afterward is something I'm not looking to repeating."

"Me, neither," he said.

He took her hand, cradling it in his own. He ran his finger over her knuckles. She felt an electric charge go up her arm and then shivers across her shoulders and chest. Her nipples tightened and her breasts felt fuller.

She remembered how one simple touch could lead to much more. She pushed her fingers through his and held his hand in hers. He tightened his grasp on her fingers and lifted her hand to his mouth.

The warmth of his breath brushed over the back of her hand. He looked up at her as he kissed her hand and then her wrist.

She pulled her hand from his grasp and put it in her lap. She wasn't ready to rekindle the sexual flame that had always been between them. Not at this instant. But to reclaim herself she knew that she was going to have to. And she was afraid that when she did she'd lose a little bit more of herself.

3

JAY LEANED BACK in his chair, lacing his fingers over his chest. Granted, she couldn't see his eyes in the growing darkness, but still she felt the weight of his gaze on her. He looked aloof and dangerous and though she knew he wouldn't hurt her she felt that he wanted to keep the world at bay.

"So…how did you start a bakery?" he asked.

"With a lot of loans from the bank," she replied with a wry grin. Her parents had offered to help by cosigning but she'd refused. After the debacle of her "marriage" to Jay she'd needed to do something on her own.

"Was it hard?" he asked.

"You have no idea," she said.

"That's why I'm asking," he said. "The woman I married was looking for a family and wanted to settle down."

"Well, that didn't work out, did it?" she asked.

She was starting to feel annoyed. She had enjoyed Jay's company, but a part of her hadn't wanted to. She wanted Jay to have turned into some kind of jerk so she could stand up and walk away. Instead he'd been nice and kept the conversation going when all she wanted was…well, some awkward silences.

"No, it didn't. So tell me, what happened? I want to know what I missed," he said.

She tried studying him. The new him. But memories of the old him were bonded deep within her. She felt vulnerable and unsure. She pulled her sunglasses off the top of her head and put them on.

"I started doing bakery competitions in the area and winning some of them. Then I was invited to be a part of *Good Morning Los Angeles*'s cooking segment and gained some notoriety that way. But there was another cupcake girl, Staci, and we kept bumping into each other. And one thing led to another until one night, after a few too many margaritas, I found myself agreeing to be her partner and open a bakery with her."

He just continued watching her and she fiddled with her fork. She didn't like his attention on her because she didn't want to feel even a bit of attraction for him. But it was crazy to try to deny it. She did want him.

There was something exciting about him—there always had been. He exuded male confidence, and he had from the moment he'd walked up to her at the roulette table and teasingly asked her for a kiss. She'd given it to him and he'd placed all his money on the table and won. He'd called her his lucky charm and spent the rest of that night and the next four days wining and dining her. He'd made her feel as if she was the most beautiful and exciting woman in the world.

And she'd heard the saying "older and wiser" but somehow, where he was concerned, she wasn't any wiser. She wanted to walk over to him, turn him away from the table and straddle his lap while she kissed him long and deep.

"Margaritas, eh?" he asked.

"I've got to lay off the margaritas," she said, trying to sound wry but knowing she just sounded a little pathetic. It was after a night of drinking one too many strawberry margaritas that she'd agreed to marry Jay.

"I don't know about that. Sweet Dreams seems to have paid off," he said. "And everyone's heard of your bakery. Although it wasn't what I'd expected."

"What did you expect?" she asked.

He shrugged and looked away from her. "I don't know. I was kind of hoping you'd be waiting for me to come back."

"You left me," she said, not able to keep the incredulity out of her voice. "And I divorced you, remember?"

"I know. It was a fantasy," he admitted. "I knew you wouldn't be. You have a very strong sense of self. I think that is part of what made me leave. You had your own dreams. Your own desires."

She nodded at him. She didn't want to travel or be a military man's wife. Her life had been rooted here in Southern California long before she'd opened Sweet Dreams.

"You surprised me, Alysse. You still do. I'm very proud of your success even though I know I have no right to be."

She picked up her glass and took a dainty mouthful of wine. Trying for an attitude of sophistication she didn't really feel at this moment. "If you hadn't left me…I wouldn't have the bakery. So I guess I owe you some thanks for that."

She hadn't gone to a therapist after what had happened but she had started reading a lot of self-help books. At first she kept waiting for him to walk back into her life and then after three months of that kind of hopelessness, she'd decided she needed to move on. All her life she'd had a plan for herself and it had always involved a white knight riding in and scooping her up on his horse. It was odd, but she'd always wanted to be lifted onto a horse by a big, strong warrior man and carried out of her dull ordinary life.

After Jay…it was clear that no white knight was coming and that her warrior man was just a man with issues and flaws. She'd also come to the realization that her man hadn't had the same dream of a life together that she'd had. So she'd had to readjust. And baking, not to mention graduating from cooking school, had helped her do that.

Now, she was self-supporting and happy with her career. She could easily see herself owning Sweet Dreams and baking for the rest of her life. That thought often made her smile when she was feeling alone.

But Jay was back and he was offering her a chance to mend her broken heart and finally reclaim a little of her feminine pride. Though she'd never admit it out loud, having him leave her the way he had had made her doubt her own attractiveness to the opposite sex. Had made her wonder if she had some kind of flaw that she'd never noticed before.

"Alysse?" he asked in that deep voice, reminiscent of the way he'd sounded on the phone this afternoon when he'd pleaded with her to deliver the dessert.

"Hmm?"

"I asked if you were done with your salad. The waiter wants to clear our plates and bring out dinner," he said.

"Yes, I am. Sorry about that," she said. She really needed to stop daydreaming and pay attention. This was Jay Michener and he wouldn't hesitate to use any weakness he spotted against her. She knew him well enough to know he was back here to win. "I was lost in the past."

"I understand that," he said. "I've spent a lot of time in the past."

The waiter cleared the table and laid down the dinner plates. He removed the covers and she saw that there was a pan-seared tuna with a creamy risotto and asparagus. It smelled heavenly and she stared at her plate, trying to make the evening about food instead of about the past. But she knew that was a lie.

The waiter offered cracked black pepper and refilled their wineglasses before leaving. She stared at the empty beach. The sun still shone but it wasn't very bright.

"Alysse?"

"Yes?" she asked. It was silly to still be wearing sunglasses, she thought as she focused on Jay's face.

"Are you okay?"

"No," she said. "I'm not. This is the most surreal night of my entire life and that's counting the night I married a stranger."

His mouth tightened but then he relaxed his shoulders. "I guess I'm glad it's not boring for you."

Just that one sentence shocked her and made her smile. Then she started laughing though it wasn't that funny and she felt the sting of tears and the very real urge to start crying. Damn. She turned her head away from him, pushed her sunglasses up on top of her head and wiped her eyes.

"You do know how to show a girl an interesting time," she said. "What have you been up to?"

"Fighting," he said. "That's what I do."

She arched one eyebrow at him. That was almost too straightforward, especially for Jay.

"Sorry. It's on a T-shirt that a guy in my unit gave me last Christmas."

"Oh," she said, realizing there was a possibility of him having a life outside the Corps. "I have one that says 'I dream in dark chocolate.'"

He smiled and they started eating. She gave Jay props for keeping the conversation light and she found him charming. Too charming as he recounted some humorous pranks he'd played on his buddies. That was how he referred to them. No names or any other identifiers.

"Why don't you call them by their name?" she asked as they were finishing up dinner.

"I don't know why, I just think of them as they are, like *sniper-scout*. He's the fourth one I've been paired with since I've been in the Corps."

"What does he do exactly?" she asked.

"He's my partner in the field. He helps me sight the target by gauging wind and other factors. He's got my back, you know?"

She shook her head. "In the movies, snipers are always loners, but it doesn't seem like you are."

He shrugged again and she noticed the way his massive shoulders moved. He was still in top form, with muscles bulging under that black T-shirt of his. "Sort of. We work in pairs but because of burnout and other issues we don't always develop deep bonds. I'd work alone if I could."

"Why?" she asked, putting her silverware down to concentrate on what he was saying. To be honest, his answer didn't surprise her. There had always been something solitary about him, even in Vegas when he'd been on leave.

"That way I don't have to depend on anyone but myself."

She tipped her head to the side to consider him. "Was that why you left me?"

"I have no idea. I've never been a coward, but walking away from you was the only thing I could do."

"Why? Because you didn't want to have to depend on me?" she asked.

"No," he said, putting his sunglasses back down over his eyes. "I didn't want you to depend on me and then let you down."

JAY DIDN'T LIKE admitting his weaknesses out loud but he knew that lying to Alysse wasn't going to win him any favors. He'd planned what he'd say and how he'd say it, but he hadn't been able to plan for her reactions.

She was hard to get a bead on tonight as she was both angry and sad and at times almost relaxed. And seeing her behavior tonight made him wonder if he should have just stayed gone. Selfishly, for his own peace of mind, he'd had to see her again.

He'd had to try to make things right. He wasn't a

complex man and Lord knew he didn't have any real idea of how a relationship should work, but having seen his buddies and their wives, Jay knew that it was possible for a guy to be a soldier and have a life outside the Corps.

"So you decided just to let me down and get it over with."

In this respect she was right, although there had been so much more to the decision. Now he was paying for it. He wondered sometimes if he'd be just better off staying to himself. His dad had always said he was a lone wolf who wasn't fit for socializing and at times like this Jay believed that. "I think we've both gone around this long enough. Tell me more about the woman you are today."

She took a swallow of her wine and then gave him a half smile. He couldn't stop staring at her mouth. She'd had some kind of lipstick on earlier, but during the meal it had worn off. And left just the natural color of her lips, which brought an image to his mind of her tight nipples.

Damn. He wanted her.

"I work, I meet friends at the beach, I go to my parents' house for dinner. I have a normal life."

"Are you happy?" he asked.

"Most of the time. What are you trying to ask me?"

"Am I screwing your life up again by coming back?" he asked, being as blunt as he could. "I didn't think that you would be so—"

She laughed quietly, and this time not with the strained quality she'd had before. "So…what?"

"So real," he said at last.

"How did you expect me to be?" she asked. Then she leaned her elbows on the table and looked him straight in the eye. "Vegas wasn't real for either of us."

"I know that now, but I didn't at the time," he admitted. He'd been seduced by the lights of Vegas and that attitude the city had of everything seeming possible. He'd felt the pull of Alysse so strongly he hadn't thought beyond his time there and having her in his arms. And that had been a mistake because he'd ignored the fact that he wasn't the kind of guy that women liked having around. His own mother had proven that point a long time ago.

Alysse put both hands on the table and continued looking at him. He knew she couldn't see his eyes but he wondered what she was searching for in his face. He knew he was very good at not giving up anything, but he still wished that maybe she'd find whatever it was she needed to see.

"Why? Even I knew it was just a fantasy," she said.

"I didn't. If I don't have a weapon in my hand and a target in my sights I don't know what's real," he explained.

She sat back in her chair and he knew he hadn't given her the answer she'd been wanting. Still, he didn't have any explanation other than the truth. "Why did you take a chance on me if you knew that Vegas was all lights and make-believe?"

She tucked a strand of her long pretty hair behind her ear and nibbled on her lower lip. "I thought...I thought that after the glitter of Vegas faded away we'd still have the connection. I thought we'd formed a bond so quickly because it *was* real."

Fair enough, he thought. Both of them were living their own fantasy and their perceptions had led to…him leaving. Not her actions, she couldn't have been more perfectly suited to him during that weekend.

"Where do we go from here?" she asked.

"We're going to date. *Real* dating. To see if our bond was real," he said.

Alysse shook her head and pushed back from the table. She paced to the edge of the cabana where she looked out at the shore. Waves gently lapped on the beach.

He stood up and walked over to her, putting his hand on her shoulder. She shrugged his hand away and he realized for the hundredth time what a monumental task he'd set for himself.

"What are you thinking?" he asked.

"That I'm not sure I can do this," she said. "I know that I have said that before but the more time I spend with you, the harder it is to remember that I have moved on."

Her words cut him, but he knew that they shouldn't. He was lucky she'd stayed for dinner. He knew each date would be a test to pass, he thought. That was motivation enough. It gave him something to focus on, something concrete that didn't make him feel so unsure.

"We *are* going to figure this out. If for no other reason than that we both need to resolve what happened."

"How do you mean?"

"I don't want to be the man who hurt you and you don't want to be the woman with the broken heart."

She pursed her lips as she turned and looked at him.

"It's the truth."

"Yes, it is. I just don't want it to be. But you're right, I need something that only you can give me, and I'm going to be ruthless about taking it, Jay. I won't make this easy for you."

He smiled and felt something tight in his chest relax. "I wouldn't want you any other way."

"Do you want me?" she asked. "Or do you just want a version of me? This isn't Vegas. I'm not going to have time to just lie in bed with you and have sex all day."

He hardened at the thought of that. That was one of his fantasies, but he also wanted more from her than the physical. Their bond had started with light flirting and kisses that he still didn't quite believe were real. No one had ever tasted as good as Alysse or had fitted into his arms just the way she did.

"Who said anything about sex?" he asked.

She closed the gap between the two of them. He held himself still as she ran her finger down the center of his chest, poking him. "This entire setup is about seduction and we both know it. So give me the truth, Marine."

He took a deep breath. "I don't know how to handle you without the sex," he said. "In bed I know what I'm doing and…well, it makes our relationship a lot easier."

"That's not a relationship," she said.

"I know. Believe me, if it was we'd still be together and the last few years would have been much different."

She smiled at him. "I don't understand you, Jay."

He didn't understand himself. This crossroads had started in the desert sand but it was turning into a crisis inside him. Something that he had to resolve, or he knew he'd end up just as bitter and lonely as his old man had been. Having a chance at happiness with Alysse—he knew he couldn't, wouldn't, give that up.

"I don't either, but we can do something about it," he said.

"You are very confident about this."

"It's the only plan I've got. I'm kind of invested in making it work."

She nodded. "Things are going to be different this time."

"I get that," he said.

"Good. I'm not the passive person I used to be."

He laughed that she said that with a straight face. "You are so far from passive. From the beginning you had me wrapped around your little finger."

"Did I?" she asked. "It felt the other way around to me."

In that instant he knew that the bond they'd formed had its grounding in something beyond just sex. He had always known it deep inside because she'd never left his thoughts even when they had half the world between them. But she'd made him very aware that the feelings weren't one-sided. And that gave him more hope than he probably deserved.

THE WAITER LIT the tiki torches near them and delivered a coffee service. She glanced at her watch, knowing she should be leaving, but she didn't want to go just yet. Jay made her feel as if this was the first day of the rest of her life.

She wanted it to be worth something. She thought about how one-sided her life had been since she'd started working at the bakery. How when she went to the beach to play volleyball with her friends and family she always felt like the odd person out because everyone else had a partner and she was afraid to risk herself again.

Jay had stolen a little of that happiness from her and she wanted it back. She wanted everything life had to offer and the only way she would get that would be to take it back.

Jay had been right when he'd said she wasn't passive. She liked to pretend she was easygoing and just went with the flow, but truly, she was determined to have everything her own way.

And maybe Jay had sensed that and he'd left her because he knew she wasn't going to be content just to let him be her lover and rule her life the way he had that week in Vegas. She had changed in the last five years and she hadn't even realized how much until she'd been sitting across from him at dinner. She wanted things now that she hadn't understood were important back then.

It was humbling to discover that though she'd felt so adult and grown up in Vegas she was only now catching on to how much she still had to learn. It had been easy to fall for Jay because she'd never really lost before. Were her expectations too high? Not high enough?

"Come back and sit down," he said.

She nodded and returned to the table. No matter how much she wanted to run away and leave him she knew she wasn't going to do it until she'd gotten some more information from him.

"What are you thinking about?"

"Just wondering how difficult the last few years have been for you," she said.

"Not too bad," he answered. "A lot of routine and discipline."

"Do you like the routine?"

"Love it. In the Corps there are rules and if you follow them you get the expected results."

"Just like baking," she said.

He chuckled and she caught her breath as she recognized just how handsome he was when he smiled. She stared at him and noticed again the new cut above his lip. Just a small scar, not recent, but it hadn't been there the last time she'd seen him.

Suddenly she had a vision of a warrior, battered and bruised, but continuing to fight because he didn't know anything else. She wondered if Jay had a code of honor and then realized what a silly thing that was to consider: she knew he had a code of honor. He'd left her to keep from hurting her.

That was what he'd said. And in a way she could see the logic in it, but in another way she didn't get it. She truly didn't understand this man.

"I guess it is like baking," he said at last. "I like the order of it."

"Me, too. But I also like coming up with my own variations. I use the recipes for the basics, then I build on them."

He shook his head. "There's little room for variation when you are fighting a war."

"I wouldn't know about that. But I think I want to. Tell me about yourself, Jay."

"There's not much to tell," he said.

She frowned. "I'm not going to let you push it aside. I need to know what you're really like."

"Fine. I wake up at five-thirty even when I'm on leave and run five miles. Then I shower and eat breakfast."

"What do you have for breakfast?" she asked, suspecting he ate the same thing every day. After all, he'd admitted he liked routine. It was just the Jay in Vegas that had been spontaneous.

"Cereal. I like it and it tastes the same wherever I am in the world."

She wanted to ask him more questions, but he seemed lost in thought. She could almost see the gears in his mind turning as he mentally went through his routine.

"I report for duty when I'm not on leave and check my weapons and get my assignment. Depending on what my mission is I follow the parameters of that. Then, at the end of the day or mission, depending on how long it lasts, I return home."

"What kind of assignments do you have?"

"You don't want to know," he said.

"Yes, I do."

"Tell me about your day," he said.

She narrowed her gaze on him. "You're stubborn. More so than I am."

"Damned straight."

She just sat there knowing that she'd play this out to the end by not budging an inch. But then if she did and kept up the stone wall around her emotions, was he going to leave her exactly the same person she was when she arrived here? Alone and not trusting any man.

"Fine. I wake up at four and hit the snooze button twice before I finally have to jump out of bed and hurry through my shower. Once I get to the bakery I am almost awake. I have a cup of coffee and start making the pastries we need for the morning. Staci gets there about the same time as I do and the first fifteen minutes are eerily quiet until we both wake up and then we start talking."

"What do you talk about?"

"Anything, everything and nothing. You know? We just talk and then the day speeds by and when it's six we close up and head home."

"That's a long day," he said.

"Yes, but I like it. We're closed on Sunday and Monday and I always wake up at four and can't go back to sleep. It's so frustrating."

He chuckled, and for a moment she forgot the past and the baggage they both had. She felt as though she was on a date, and she relaxed for the first time in more than five years.

"I hate that."

"Does it happen to you?" she asked.

He shook his head and she had to laugh. It figured. He was the kind of man who was too regimented ever to have that kind of sleeping issue. He probably ordered his body to exercise and it did it.

But he wasn't a machine, no matter how much he might seem so on the surface. She knew that he was a man and he wanted—no, needed—something from her. Some sign that there was more to life than what he'd known, and she was so afraid to go down this path with him.

But she wasn't about to let herself chicken out.

4

JAY DIDN'T BELIEVE in luck. He'd seen too many guys with four-leaf-clover tattoos leaving in body bags to think that there was anything in this world that could influence his fate. He'd kind of always known he made his own luck and sitting across from Alysse on the beach with the waves crashing on the shore...well, it was about as lucky as he'd ever felt.

Tonight he'd realized how little he knew Alysse and that had maybe been why he'd left. Perhaps that panicked sweat he'd woken up in the last morning he'd been in Vegas had had nothing to do with her large family and the expectations she had for him, and everything to do with the fact that he didn't really know her outside of that king-size bed they'd shared.

He wanted to believe that. Truly, he did. But at the end of the day he'd taken one look at the sweetly sleeping woman and known deep in his soul he was going to hurt her. So he'd done it the quickest way possible. Got it over with and got out.

But then that damned IED had changed his life. And now he was back trying to carve something from the past that he should never have given up. It wasn't as simple as reliving what they'd had because they couldn't go back. He wanted to know if he could have the life he'd never experienced with her.

"So tell me about your near miss," she said in a careful tone.

Alysse was the prettiest girl he'd ever known. He'd seen beautiful women before but there was something about her that had drawn him from the moment their eyes had met. And sitting across from her now, he was still enamored with her. She had mellowed toward him during dinner, though he knew he was still on the hot seat and she'd walk away from him without looking back.

"There's not much to tell. The logistics of it won't matter to you. Just know that I was lying in the sand, sun in my eyes and for a minute I thought I was dying. In that instant it came to me that I had no one. It sharpened all of my desires and all of my ideas of what life was about."

She reached over and rubbed her hand down his arm, taking his fingers in her grasp and squeezing them gently. "I'm sorry you were alone."

He nodded and looked away. Even though the sun had started to set, he'd kept his sunglasses on so she couldn't read his emotions or see the fear he knew was in his eyes. She was too good for him, he thought, the way she was upset about him being alone even though he'd tossed her aside.

"It's my own fault."

"Yes, it is," she said. "So you almost died and thought you needed someone to mourn you?"

"Nah. I almost died and I thought, Really, man, this is all you want out of life?" Faced with his own mortality, he'd acknowledged he wanted more than what he had. Yet he wasn't too sure what he'd do with more if he got it.

The one thing he was sure of was that Alysse was the key to understanding that. She truly was the only woman he'd spent more than one night with. But he wasn't about to tell her that. She was looking skeptical enough about his entire proposition.

"What answer did you find?" she asked.

"I haven't. But the last time I was happy outside of the Corps was with you, so…"

"I can't believe you," she said, shaking her head. "You're back here hoping for something."

"That *is* what I said," he reminded her gently.

She withdrew her hand from his.

He looked away and then pushed his hands through his hair. He'd rather face an entire unit of well-trained guerillas than this woman. The fact that he was still scared of her after all this time made him realize that there was more to Alysse than sex. He wanted more from her than physical pleasure, though that was still a big part of why he was here.

"I get that you are afraid to trust me, Alysse. I know that I don't deserve the slightest kindness from you—"

"Don't. Don't say things like that because you make me want to feel sorry for you," she said. "And that's not right."

He stepped toward her. "Let's go. I need to get away from here. I feel exposed."

She nodded. He saw her long hair blowing in the

wind and he had the feeling that he'd said the wrong thing. But at this point there was nothing else he could say.

"I can't…I'm not sure I can do much more tonight. I guess you can call me tomorrow," she said backing away.

He knew he had to let her go. At least until he figured out what he wanted from her and for her, as well as how to have peace in the future.

But that wasn't about to happen tonight. He knew better than that. "Can I give you a ride home?"

"No. I have my car," she said. "Thanks for dinner."

"Hey, I'm not about to let you treat this like some casual date. I want to know what you are feeling."

"Feeling? I have no idea what I feel at this moment. I'm scared and nervous and excited. I don't have any idea what will happen next and I'm not entirely sure that I'm not making a stupid decision because…well, because I never actually got over you, Jay."

"That's good," he said, feeling more confident than he had since she'd arrived on the beach.

"I'm glad you think so. But you are here to sort out your life and I already have one. One that you didn't want to be a part of."

"We don't know that. This second chance—"

"Is for you," she said. "It's not for me and I have to remember that. I'm not going to let you hurt me again."

The very last thing he wanted was to hurt Alysse, but he wasn't about to let his chance—his chance at… what?—go. He had no idea what she going to be to him, though his gut said she was his golden ticket and a man didn't get too many of those.

"I get that," he said. "Thanks for staying for dinner."

"You're welcome," she replied, making ready to leave. Then he noticed the Sweet Dreams bakery box.

"Dessert!" he said. That was the excuse he'd used to get her down here and maybe now it would be reason enough for her to stay. He could only hope so.

"Dessert?" she asked.

"We haven't had whatever you brought for us yet," he said. "You can't leave until we have dessert."

With an almost sad look on her face, she pushed her sunglasses to the top of her head and he saw her pretty blue eyes. Saw the pain and fear she'd alluded to earlier and he knew he was a goner. He was never going to be able to make an unbiased decision where she was concerned.

He was alive but not well and he wanted to take care of himself and find out if he had any chance at life, a real life, but he wasn't going to be able to put himself before her.

"Please," he said at last, because any other words were beyond him.

She blinked and then nodded. "We have to get past this."

"I know," he said. "You're afraid I'm going to hurt you and I'd rather die than do that."

"You can't be vulnerable to me," she said slowly. "If you are…we will both lose."

"This isn't about winning," he said, closing the gap between them and pulling her into his arms. "This is about…"

She tipped her head back and put her hands on his shoulders. Going up on tiptoe she leaned up and brushed her lips over his. Then she slowly opened her mouth and her tongue sneaked out to touch his and he melted.

He forgot that he didn't want to screw this up and went with his gut. And his gut said this woman belonged in his arms. She belonged with him.

ALYSSE KNEW SHE'D MADE a huge mistake by coming here. She'd already been in a "romantic" mood, thinking that this Marine was going to make a gesture that would win back his woman. Being the woman in question…well, a cupcake wasn't enough, but sadly Jay was. He was the guy she'd been waiting for and now she found she was ready.

Her control of the kiss lasted briefly and then Jay's hands were on her hips and he pulled her off balance and into him. She wrapped her arms around his shoulders and was overcome with an emotion that was embarrassing. She felt the sting of tears so abruptly she stopped the kiss and rested her head on his shoulder.

It had been too long. She took a deep shuddering breath. She refused to cry. But she couldn't help it when he slid one hand up her back to her neck and rubbed her shoulders.

"Ah, Aly. I'm so sorry."

"Me, too," she admitted, the truth finally revealing itself. Jay wasn't someone she could be casual about, as he'd said. If she couldn't walk away now and not look back, she was never going to be able to do it.

She might want to pretend that she had some say over her emotions, but truthfully she didn't, not where he was concerned.

He tipped her chin up, looking down at her with those big dark chocolate-brown eyes of his and he kissed her. His hands framed her face as his mouth moved over hers with the confidence and surety she remembered.

But then his tongue slid against hers and she stopped thinking. She just let her feelings take over. Shivers spread down her spine. Her breasts felt full and needy. She shifted her shoulders to rub against him and he moaned deep in his throat as he widened his stance so that his hips cradled hers.

She felt the nudge of his cock as he hardened and she moaned a little as he rubbed himself against her.

She was alive and nothing else mattered to her in that moment. Jay's hands were under her shirt and sliding over her back. His big calloused hands caressed up and down her spine until she was arching against him, trying to get even closer.

He lifted her off her feet and took a few steps before sitting down on the closest chair. She straddled him and looked down at him, smiling.

"I want you," he said. He took the tip of his finger and drew it down the center of her throat and then caressed the skin where her neck and throat met. It was a particularly sensitive spot for her and she shuddered with awareness.

"I can tell," she said, rocking her hips over his erection.

"I never could hide the way you make me feel," he said.

"I'm glad," she said. She didn't want to talk. If they did, she'd start thinking and worrying and she'd have to leave. And right now she was remembering that it had been a very long time since any man had touched her this way.

She leaned down, dropped nibbling kisses against his jaw, and slowly worked her way to his lips. When she met his mouth, he tunneled his fingers through her hair and tangled his tongue with hers. She shifted on his lap and knew she was close to climaxing.

She reached between them, running her hands over his chest encased in that black T-shirt. He was a fine-looking man, she thought. She reached for the hem of the shirt and lifted it up and over his head.

She sat on his thighs and looked down at the light smattering of hair on his chest. The muscles pulsed as she moved her touch over him.

She traced the line of hair that narrowed over his hard stomach before it disappeared into the waistband of his jeans where flesh met fabric. His stomach tightened and he let out a long, low breath.

"Damn, woman…"

"Like that?" she asked, feeling a heady sense of power over him. This was what she'd wanted. She needed to be in control.

"Love it."

"Good," she said, shifting on his lap to lean forward and kiss his chest. She kissed each pec and then used her tongue on his brown nipples. Gooseflesh spread down his body wherever she touched him.

His hands tightened on her waist and then he swept his hands up her back, taking off her shirt. He tossed it to the side and brought his hands around to her breasts. He cupped them and leaned into her.

She felt the arousing warmth of his breath on her skin before the brush of his lips. He kissed the scalloped edge of her lacy bra over one breast and then the other. She shuddered on his lap, fighting to control the sensations that threatened to overtake her.

He put his hands around her midriff and then brushed his thumbs up until he found the center of her nipple under the lacy fabric of her bra. Using his thumbs, he stroked back and forth and she found his mouth.

His tongue sucked hers strongly, and again she shuddered. Frustrated by her jeans and his, she wished they were both naked. She needed more from him and she needed it now.

She reached for his zipper, but he stopped her. "Not yet."

"Why not?"

"I want this to last."

"I don't think I can wait," she confessed. She was on the edge of coming just from this little bit of temptation and she didn't want to draw it out. She wanted to take her orgasm now.

"It will be worth your while," he said.

She smiled. The sound of his words affected her as much as his touch did. He unhooked her bra with a quick flick of his wrist. The cups stayed in place on her breasts and she saw him glance down at her.

She felt his cock twitch against her, and knew the sight of her breasts had turned him on. She reached behind her to brace her hands on the table so she could lean back and give him a better view.

"Aly, you are gorgeous," he said, his words low, husky.

"Am I?"

"Hell, yeah. I'm almost afraid to touch you. Afraid to let you touch me because I'll wake up and find out this is just another fantasy."

His words were penetrating. She didn't want to find out this wasn't real either. And she needed this night. The fantasy of Jay and this moment.

She brought her hand up and covered his lips with her fingers. "Don't talk. Just make love to me, Jay. Make me forget everything but this."

He put both hands over her breasts and slowly peeled back the lacy cups. He stopped when the areole of her left breast was revealed and leaned in to tongue the fabric out of the way. He teased it with his mouth and then slowly closed his lips around her nipple.

Alysse felt her arms tremble and then a minute later, Jay's arm was around her to support her while he pleasured her. She slowly slipped a hand to touch him while he continued to caress her breasts.

She undid the button at the top of his jeans and gradually lowered the zipper, caressing him through the barrier of his boxers. He shifted his hips and she gripped his cock. It was hot and hard and she slid her hand up and down its length until his hips bucked forward and a drop of moisture was at her fingertip. She rubbed it over the head of his cock and then stroked him again.

He found the fastening of her jeans and undid them. She moved, trying to get her pants off but it wasn't going to happen while she was sitting on his lap. She pushed herself to her feet and shimmied out of her jeans and then turned back to him.

"I can't believe we're here. Like this. After everything that's happened," he said. He reached out and trailed his fingers down her stomach and around her belly button. Then his touch moved lower and he cupped her intimately.

His fingers gently stroked against her most sensitive flesh. She wanted—no needed—more and she wouldn't be denied any longer. She pushed against his shoulders, urging him back to his chair but he shook his head.

"No way. I've dreamed of this moment for too long," he said.

She was taken aback at his words. Soon she felt his mouth against her shoulder, kissing and suckling as he continued along her arm. He kept that one hand between her legs, fingers teasing her, as his other hand slipped her bra away.

His eyes narrowed intensely as his gaze fixed on her exposed torso. She splayed her hands on his chest and, in a reverent way, opened his jeans. She pushed them down his legs along with his boxers. He stepped carefully out of them while continuing to explore her body with his mouth.

She touched his cock. He stopped then, and lifted her up to carry her. She put her arm around his shoulders to steady herself as he strode to the table. He set her on her feet next to it. Then he walked around the gazebo and lowered the curtains so that no one could see in. She watched every movement, admiring his fluid grace.

"Like what you see?" he asked when they were closed off from the world.

"Very much," she admitted.

"Good," he said. He returned to her side and kissed her. His hands were on her waist and he raised her up onto the table. She felt a little uncertain, but when he stepped between her legs and she felt the hot nudge of the tip of his cock she stopped worrying. She knew this was right.

He cupped her bottom and drew her closer. She responded, wrapping her legs around his hips, but he pushed them down and away. Instead, he took her hands in his and placed them on the table on either side of her. "Lean back."

She did and her breasts jutted out, as if on display, her nipples painfully tight. He leaned down and kissed each nipple, scraping briefly, carefully with his teeth before he nibbled his way down to her stomach. His tongued dipped into her belly button, readying her instantly. Then he nibbled her hip bone before gently tonguing his way to her center.

She felt his fingers first, then the brush of his tongue against her clit. She screamed his name and immediately put her hands to his head. She needed to touch him as he found that sweet bud of passion and sucked on it. She knew she was close to climaxing as soon as the tip of his finger penetrated her and the rolling wave of her orgasm began to wash over her.

Eagerly, her body responded, desperate for more. He lifted his head.

She stared down at him. "Take me, Jay."

He nodded and reached for his jeans. She saw him draw out a condom from his pocket. He opened the package and put the protection on quickly before returning to her.

He spread her legs and then she felt him tap her clit with his cock. She shivered as he rubbed himself against her and then she caught her breath as the tip of his cock entered her. But he paused there and she shifted under him, trying to get all of him.

"Beg me," he said.

"Please…take me, Jay."

He slid another tiny inch inside of her. "That's not begging," he said, leaning forward so that his chest teased her tingling breasts.

He whispered naughty, dirty sexual ideas in her ear and her muscles clenched around him. She felt his hips jerk, and she bit the lobe of his ear.

She could sense the shiver that went through him and then a moment later he filled her completely. She tightened her legs around his waist as he took her, relentlessly moving in and out of her body.

"Come for me," he said.

She was already from the moment he'd first thrust inside her. What control she had left was quickly slipping away. Her clit was pulsing as one sensation after another claimed her. He leaned down and kissed and sucked the side of her neck as his hips pistoned forward. On a breathy cry, her name passed his lips, and she felt his hard, smooth cock spilling into her.

Alysse ran her hand up and down his strong back and buried her face against his chest. His breath sawed in and out of his body and she relished the afterglow.

He held her loosely in his arms and then brought her to the chair with him where he'd cradled her earlier. He held her to him and she let him. She rested her head against his chest and pretended she was never going to have to leave this spot.

She wanted to stay with him, like this, and remember that one perfect week they'd spent in each other's arms.

But that wasn't going to happen. She sat up and faced him.

His expression went from relaxed and sated to guarded. "I guess that was a mistake?"

She shook her head. "Not at all. But I think that's all we are ever going to have."

"Sex? It's more than sex, Aly."

She frowned and got to her feet. She felt vulnerable and raw as she moved around gathering up her clothes, dressing as quickly as she could. She heard Jay behind her, dressing as well, and by the time she turned around he was fully clothed and looking every inch the Marine that he was.

This wasn't the sexy, demanding lover of only minutes ago. This was the man who'd called her down here with a mission in mind. She had the feeling that lovemaking hadn't been his objective.

"I want more than sex. It wasn't some hot lover I

was missing when I was lying in the desert sand feeling like I was going to die."

"Who were you missing?"

"You."

"You had me," she said, trying to objectify what had just happened so it wouldn't mean as much to either of them.

"I did. I made a mistake. I'm trying to make up for that."

She laughed because he sounded so wounded and so…well, not like himself. "You said sex was the only place we communicated honestly."

"I was a guy looking to get laid when I said that."

She raised her shoulder and tipped her head to the side. "Isn't that who you were tonight?"

"No."

She arched her eyebrow at him.

"Well, yes, but I want more. Dammit, Aly, nothing is going the way I planned."

"Welcome to the real world, Marine. It's not like the Corps where there are rules and everyone follows them."

He stalked over to her and put his hands on her waist and lifted her off her feet to kiss her. She could have ignored it if it was hard and demanding, but instead it was soft, seductive. It was every tender feeling she had burning inside her, waiting to get out.

She almost put her arms around him, yet she knew she had to get away. She needed to get some distance between them or he was going to have his willing little Vegas-minded sex-crazy wife back. And she wasn't that woman.

Really, she assured herself. Tonight was her chance to have Jay one last time before she set about curing herself of caring about him. Curing herself from wanting that hot body of his pressed against her again. Curing herself of the broken heart that she'd never been able to heal.

5

"THE REAL WORLD?" he said, grasping her hand and stopping her before she got too far away. "I know more about reality than you do. You are about to go happily back to your safe, happy life never knowing what I've done to keep you secure."

"That's not what I meant. You think you can plan out every detail and I'll just fall in line like a good little girl."

"God knows that you are a good girl, aren't you?" he asked sarcastically.

She stopped abruptly. He knew he was pushing her into a corner. He didn't care. He felt so out of control right now he wanted to see her lose it a little, too.

"I always have been, but then following the rules didn't exactly help me out with my marriage," she said.

"I never intended to hurt you," he said.

"Well, you can't be blamed then for your actions, is that it?" she asked.

He pushed his hands through his short-cropped hair and realized this conversation was on a downward spiral. "No, that's not what I meant."

"What did you mean? You have no defense, you walked away and left me and now you're back… I'm entitled to be angry."

"Yes, you are," he said, letting his own anger abate. He knew Alysse hadn't meant that the way he'd taken it.

"Come on, let's go back to my room and we can talk about it. This isn't the place for us to do that and we have too much to hash out."

"No," she said as she deliberately pulled her hand free. "I don't think we have anything more to say to each other."

"Why not?" he asked, but he already suspected he knew the answer.

From the second they'd met in Vegas he'd promised her the world to get her into his room and kept her there as long as he could. Not just because of the physical pleasure but because in his room, when it was just the two of them, he could keep the real world at bay. The reality that spoke of the group of friends she had who wanted them to go clubbing or gaming with them. The reality that spoke of the community of people that she surrounded herself with. The reality that spoke the truth—that he didn't really fit in her life.

"Jay, I don't want to hurt your feelings but you have to know that I had sex with you tonight to regain my ego, the ego you bruised so badly when you left me. I needed to prove to myself that you still wanted me."

"Ah, hell…"

He could see the slight red abrasion that his beard had left on her neck. "That about sums it up."

He had wanted tonight to be the romance he needed

to get back into her life and he feared that once again he'd underestimated the parameters of this mission.

"I'd say I'm sorry but I don't think it would help," he said at last.

"You're right. I know you're searching for answers for your future and I get that, believe me, I do. But for me, right now, I need to… I just need to figure out some things about myself."

Jay looked at this woman and knew that if any other girl were standing there he'd write tonight off as a one-night stand and let her go. But this was Alysse. The one woman in the world who had haunted his dreams for the last five years, and somehow, if she needed to use him, well, then he was okay with it.

"So you want to use me for sex?" he asked, a teasing note in his voice that he hoped would mask his own desperation for her not to dismiss him. Sex was the one place in his relationship with her where he felt secure.

Finally, he understood a little of what she must be feeling and he was humbled by her courage. The fact that she must feel at least a hint of what he felt and she'd stayed and had dinner with him anyway…well, that spoke to him.

"Leave it to you to boil it down to sex," she said. "But yes, I am going to use you to figure out why I don't want another man to touch me, why I haven't been able to go on more than one date with any guy. I'm stuck and I'm ready to move on."

He nodded. It was a gamble he was taking and he knew that. What he didn't know was if Alysse would ever be able to really forgive him. And what about a future for them? Was that even possible? After everything he'd been through, could he stay here and live some kind of normal suburban life? For now though, he could help her out and maybe figure himself out at the same time.

"Okay."

"Okay?" she asked.

"I'll let you use me for sex."

"Oh, Jay. I wish it were that easy," she said. "I'm going to use you to get over you."

Jay pulled her into his arms because she looked so small, so fragile, standing there and he needed to touch her. Really touch her, not just hold her hand. He hugged her and ran his hands up and down her back and then leaned away to see her eyes.

"You are going to get over Vegas Jay who wasn't ready for you," he said. "But I am a different man today, Aly, and I'm not letting you go."

She pulled away from him and adjusted the strap of her purse on her shoulder as the cool evening breeze stirred her long ginger hair. She studied him for what felt like an eternity.

"I'm not sure that I'm going to give you the chance to keep me," she said. "You're going to have to prove you're worthy of me this time."

She walked away then and all he could do was watch her leave. He understood the path he'd started down was going to be hard and fraught with obstacles but he did know one thing with utter certainty. He wasn't about to back down from this.

For the first time since he'd lain in that hospital in Afghanistan he felt truly alive, and he had Alysse to thank for that. He knew that had to mean something important and he was determined to understand what.

She wasn't about to make it easy for him and he knew he didn't want easy. He wanted a path to lead him to answer what she meant to him.

FOR ONCE SHE HAD no problems getting out of bed at 4:00 a.m. Considering she'd tossed and turned all night it was a relief when the alarm went off and she jumped out of bed. Alysse took a quick shower and stared at herself in the mirror as she put on her makeup. She looked tired and tense. Last night had been…

Don't think about it, she ordered herself as she went out to her VW convertible and drove to work. There wasn't a lot of traffic on the road at this time of the morning, which was a good thing because her mind was definitely not on the road. Instead she thought about last night and hoped against hope that she hadn't made a huge mistake.

But she suspected she had. She'd let lust rule and now she was regretting it. She shouldn't have slept with Jay because objectivity had left him. *Ha,* she thought. Objectivity had left her a long time before they'd had sex together.

She unlocked the back door of the bakery and let herself in. She grabbed a cup of French roast from the Keurig machine and got started on the Danish dough. But that didn't distract her because she could do the morning baking on autopilot and all she could think of was last night and Jay.

It didn't matter that she thought she'd made a huge

mistake. A part of her wanted to see him again and only regretted that she hadn't stayed and slept in his arms.

She groaned out loud. What was wrong with her? Was she destined to be a fool forever where Jay was concerned?

"You okay?"

Alysse jumped and turned to face the doorway where Staci stood. The other woman looked just as sleepy as Alysse felt. But she went straight to work on her morning baking.

"Yes. Why?" Alysse asked. She was having lunch with her mom later today and if she couldn't fool Staci into thinking nothing was up, then she didn't stand a chance with her mom.

"You have been staring at the flour for about five minutes, and unless you are trying to use your mind power to make the Danishes this morning…"

Alysse dumped the flour into the mixer and then added the other dry ingredients. She cursed under her breath as she realized she hadn't sifted the dry stuff together. She had to get her head into baking and off a certain good-looking Marine.

"Sorry. I'm not myself today."

"Are you getting sick?" Staci said. "If you are, I can handle this and you can head back home."

"No, I'm fine. I'm just a little off my game."

"Good. Because I want to hear about the guy last night," Staci said. She started pulling things from the pantry area and bringing them to her own station. "Was he the big romantic you thought he'd be?"

"Ha, no," Alysse replied.

"Sorry he was a dud. Did he pay you?" Staci asked.

Given everything that had happened last night she'd forgotten about charging Jay for the cupcake. She included that on his list of offenses.

"It was a setup, Staci. I never told you but I'm divorced. And the guy was my ex-husband. I never thought I'd see him again."

Staci was staring at her as if she'd grown a second head or maybe really had created Danishes with just her mind power. She should have kept that special nugget to herself, Alysse thought. But Jay had rattled her. She had no idea if using him was going to help her out or if she was out for revenge, even though that wasn't her style.

"Sorry. Forget I said that. Let's get the baking done," she said, eyeing the butter she'd need next.

"Oh, hell, no," Staci said, coming over to Alysse's station. "You can't drop a bombshell like that and then say never mind. I want details."

Alysse paused and leaned back against the counter. Maybe talking to Staci would help. Although logically, she already knew what she should do—never see Jay again. "Like what?"

"Let's start with your marriage," Staci said. "But we have to work while we talk or we won't be able to open on time."

Her friend returned to her station and picked up where she'd left off. That she was being so matter-of-fact enabled Alysse to regain her equilibrium. She knew she had to work, the bakery's fate rested on the two of them getting their products made each morning.

"We met and married in Vegas and spent a fabulous week in the honeymoon suite of the Golden Dream

Hotel. When I woke up on the day we were supposed to go home, he was gone. No note, nothing. Just disappeared."

"Oh, my God. That's… How did you cope with it?" Staci asked. "I would have hunted his ass down and reamed him a new one."

"He's a Marine…a warrior. He'd be hard to take in a fight." To be honest, that had been part of what had drawn her to Jay. Being athletic she was hard-pressed to find a guy much better than her at most sports and one who didn't treat her like one of the guys. From the beginning Jay had treated her as though she was special—a lady.

"I don't care. What did you do?" Staci asked again. She had all of her ingredients assembled.

"I channeled that anger into baking and beating you at regional competitions," Alysse said. She flipped on her mixer to combine the wet and dry ingredients. Staci did the same, but came over to her.

"Because you are in pain I'm going to let you get away with saying you always beat me," she said, giving Alysse a quick hug before going back to her station.

Alysse realized then that she hadn't shut out everyone when Jay had hurt her. Just men. She'd formed this bond with Staci and she was close to her brother's girlfriend, too.

She and Staci removed their dough from the mixers and started rolling it out. One of the things that Alysse loved most about baking was how she could take a bunch of separate things and make them into something whole. Something good. She liked seeing the dough form.

"So what happened then?" Staci asked.

"I divorced him while he was on tour in Iraq. He signed the papers and my attorney said he reenlisted but went to Afghanistan this time. I have tried to put him out of my mind but I don't know that I was too successful."

"Given the string of lackluster dates you've been on, I'd say you haven't been. So why's he back?" Staci asked.

Alysse paid close attention to the individual Danishes she was starting to create on her baking sheets. She went to the refrigerator to get the different fruits that she had prepared last night while she'd been waiting for Jay's cake to bake.

"I don't know," she said.

She didn't want to tell Staci he wanted her back and was determined to win her over. She didn't want Staci to know how weak she was where Jay was concerned and that she was contemplating letting him into her life, considering how badly he'd hurt her.

"Yeah, right."

Staci was preparing croissants and had set the dough aside to rise, now she moved on to the doughnuts.

"Did you sleep with him?" Staci asked in a low voice.

"Staci!"

"Well?"

Alysse bit her lower lip. "I'm not going to answer that."

"That means you did. You still want him. Do you still love him?" Staci persisted.

"I don't know. I think he's the reason all my dates

have sucked so much and I want to be able to move on. I'm still not sure I can trust him or myself. He's come back to figure out if he can have a life outside the Corps and apparently he wants me to be a part of it."

Alysse wasn't too sure that was really what Jay was after, but that was what he'd said. She trusted him to a certain extent but it was hard to see him as the settled-down type. He hadn't been four years ago; had what happened in the Middle East really changed him?

"That's great for him, but what do you want?" Staci asked. "I don't know that guy, but you do. I'm not going to judge you."

"I thought I was over him," Alysse said.

It had been really disheartening last night to admit she wasn't. She'd thought she had better self-preservation skills than that. "He broke my heart and I should have moved on, but he's still there in the back of my mind and I judge every guy I meet by the man he was in Vegas."

"Not the man he is today?"

She shrugged. "I'm not really sure who he is. I don't know that he knows either. I'm telling myself that I'm going to see him and sort out how to..."

"Hurt him?" Staci supplied.

She shook her head. "I thought so, but I couldn't do it. I just want to be able to move on with my life. I want to enjoy being single and I can't until I know what it is about Jay that makes me like him."

"I hope it's that easy," Staci said.

She did, too, but if the sleepless night she'd spent was any indication, nothing was going to be easy about this thing with Jay.

JAY RAN ALONG the beach and tried to clear his mind. Frankly though, there wasn't a safe place for it to go. He'd already scanned the area in front and behind him. It didn't matter that he was in San Diego on Coronado Island, a part of him just couldn't relax. The other part of his mind kept replaying last night—every damned second of it. Physical exhaustion had seemed like the only means out of the endless cycle of images of Alysse, but it wasn't. His room felt like a prison when he got back there and he wondered what normal people did on vacations. He couldn't imagine spending too much time in this place. He felt boxed-in and edgy.

He showered and changed and got on his bike and drove without a destination in mind, but he wasn't too shocked when he found himself parked down the street from Sweet Dreams. It was the one place he wanted to be. But he knew that he couldn't just show up at her bakery. She was working and he had commitments of his own.

He was meeting Lucien at ten this morning and he decided that had to be his priority right now. But Alysse was winning the battle in his mind. He had let things go too far last night and, as hard as it was for him to admit, making love to her might have actually hurt his chances of getting back together with her.

He cast aside the disturbing thought, put his sunglasses on and roared away from the curb. He drove to the offices of Company B. The name gave Jay a chuckle since Lucien and the other men who'd formed it were all from Bravo or B Company. He parked the bike and entered the impressive office building, feeling the cool air conditioning brush over his skin. The receptionist was a pretty California blonde.

She smiled up at him and Jay wondered why everything couldn't be as uncomplicated as this girl. Why hadn't he just taken those divorce papers from Alysse and moved on?

"Can I help you, sir?"

"I'm Jay Michener, I have an appointment this morning with Lucien DuPoin."

"I'll let Lucien know. Please have a seat over there. Can I get you anything to drink?"

"I'm good," Jay said. He moved toward the guest chairs but they were lined up against the glass windows and there was no way he was sitting with his back to the street. Didn't matter where he was, he couldn't switch off his instincts.

Instead he walked to an interior wall that had the Company B logo on it and their mission statement— Securing What's Important to You.

Vague, Jay thought. No clue as to what the company actually did, which was exactly as it should be.

"Jay, buddy," Lucien DuPoin greeted him.

Lucien was six feet tall, with more muscles than seemed humanly possible. His head was shaved and he wore a mustache that Jay knew hid a scar on his upper lip.

Lucien held out his hand to Jay. Jay took the hand and leaned in to bump chests with Lucien. They'd served together on Jay's third tour. "What's up?"

"Not much. Glad to see your ugly mug," Lucien replied. "How'd your plans go last night?"

"Not as I'd expected."

"What do you think of the place?" Lucien asked.

"Cushy setup you have here. Not bad for a guy from the First," Jay said. They'd served together in the First Recon Battalion in 2006.

"You have no idea," Lucien said. "Come on back and I'll show you what we're all about."

Jay followed his friend down the corridor to a high-tech, windowless conference room. Jay heard the solid thump of a bulletproof door closing behind him. There was a video wall along the right side of the room, and on the left, a huge Company B logo was displayed.

"Have a seat," Lucien said, gesturing to the leather armchairs around the table.

Jay sat down. He took his sunglasses off and set them on the table in front of him.

"Let me tell you a little about what we do and what we can offer you," Lucien said.

"Who are 'we'?"

"Myself and four other guys—two of them were Army Rangers—you met them yesterday at the bar, one was a SEAL and the other is ex-CIA. We are a unique private security force and we operate as a team or unit the way we would in the Corps. That much would be the same. We want you to be a sniper but you won't be working with a scout—we don't have the staff for that."

"What kind of missions are you taking?"

"High-risk, high-pay missions from the private sector."

"Really?"

"Yes, usually we protect or rescue ordinary citizens when our government can't go in and do so. The families or companies have the money to afford us," Lucien said.

"Like who?"

"Usually executives kidnapped in South America or kids who go missing or land in trouble. We've had a few jobs that involved the DEA and Border Patrol, but to be honest I think we've all agreed those aren't our favorites."

Jay chuckled. "I can understand that."

"Your role, if you choose to join us, would be to use the skills you have now, mainly as a marksman," Lucien explained.

Jay was one of the top-rated marksmen in the world.

"Okay. I'd be the sniper. How often do you need one?" Jay asked. Rescue missions didn't always require a man with his skills.

"More often than you'd guess," Lucien said. "T-bone, the SEAL, is good with long-range shots, but he's not you. And we need him in other roles. You'd provide expert cover. If you decide to come on board you'd be paid a monthly salary plus a bonus based on the danger factor of the mission."

The amount that Lucien mentioned was eye-opening; Jay had had no idea his skills with a weapon were worth that much. But he was looking for a change in lifestyle, not just his income bracket. "How often would I be gone? And what would I do when we aren't on a mission?"

Lucien leaned back in his chair. "We monitor security and provide bodyguards for the affluent in Southern California. Also, when dignitaries are visiting we're usually the detail assigned to guard them. So that keeps us busy. You'd have two days off a week, unless we are on a mission, and you would work regular hours."

"Sounds tempting," Jay said. Really tempting. It would mean closing one chapter of his life and starting another. Here. This job would give him a way to romance Alysse and do it right this time. But he hadn't stayed in one place since he'd left North Texas. And he had a really hard time picturing himself in a home.

"Good, I want you on my team, Jay," Lucien said.

"When do you need to know if I'm in?" Jay asked.

"When are you due to re-up?" Lucien asked.

"Two weeks. I'm on leave until then."

"Why don't you think it over tonight and let me know tomorrow?" Lucien said. "Then you can come and work with us for a few days, see if it's really what you want. I'd hate to have you regret leaving the Corps."

"Do you regret it? I thought you were going to be a lifer," Jay said.

"At first I hated it. I just wasn't cut out for civilian life, but then, once I got involved with these guys at Company B, I found my place. It's helped me a lot to be able to still use my skills but to sleep in my own bed each night," Lucien said. "Plus I have a steady woman in my life. She's more important than the Corps. For a while I didn't think she would be. Oh, I'm making a mess of saying this."

"Nah, I get it. Women are complicated," Jay said.

"You spoke a mouthful," Lucien said with his smooth Cajun accent, and Jay smiled. They'd had a lot of fun in the old days even when they were on missions, and there was something about working with his friend again that appealed to him.

"I'll call you tomorrow and let you know what I think," Jay said.

He left the offices a few minutes later and drove toward the Hotel Del Coronado but that wasn't really where he wanted to go. He wanted to see Alysse again, and if nothing else, at least talk to her.

Lucien's offer sat squarely in the front of Jay's mind. He wasn't convinced he'd be happy on a security detail, but if he knew he'd be coming home to Alysse each night, maybe he could be.

6

THE END OF THE LUNCH HOUR signaled the end of their busy time at the bakery. During the school year they'd sometimes have a rush of after-school moms and kids, but it was summertime and the afternoons were slow-paced. Staci was in the kitchen trying to perfect a recipe she'd been juggling with for days. It was a main course, not a dessert.

Alysse was afraid sometimes that Staci was getting restless in the bakery. One of her greatest fears was that Staci would move on and leave Alysse alone with Sweet Dreams. She knew she could handle the shop, but she had come to really depend on having her friend around.

But that worry wasn't foremost today, she thought, as she cleaned the counter in the empty shop front.

Okay, so she'd gotten the usual professions of love from men who liked her baked goods. However, today it hadn't seemed as much fun as it always did. She'd had a hard time flirting, knowing that Jay was back. Since their divorce had been final he'd been in the far recesses of her mind. But last night had changed all of that.

Meanwhile, her brother had called and invited her to join him and a group of their friends for a bonfire on the beach later tonight. She'd started to make her usual excuses but then decided to go. What was she going to do? Stay home and stew over Jay?

The doorbell tinkled as someone entered the shop. "Welcome to Sweet Dreams…"

Jay.

He stood backlit by the summer sun, looking totally out of place in her shop. He had on a pair of faded skin-tight jeans, a form-fitting khaki T-shirt and, despite the heat outside, a leather jacket. His aviator sunglasses were on so she couldn't see those dark chocolate eyes of his.

Why was he here? This was her Jay-free zone. She didn't want to talk to him or see him right now and certainly not in her shop.

"Why are you here?" she asked, knowing she didn't sound hospitable but not really caring. She was tired from last night, edgy about Staci's future plans and he was the source of a lot of her unease about her own future.

"I wanted to talk to you," he said as he stepped into the shop and removed his sunglasses. He opened up the side of his jacket and put them in an inner pocket. "I don't have any other number for you."

"Oh. Right." She wasn't ready to deal with Jay. Not now. Possibly not ever.

She wished she could be cool and calm, instead she figured she was coming off as more than a little flaky.

Get it together, she admonished herself.

"So, what's up?"

"I think we still need to talk. And I didn't feel comfortable about the way you left last night," he said.

"I can't really do that here because if I have a customer they have to be my priority." Thank God. The last thing she wanted to do was rehash last night and her bold proclamation that she was using him for sex.

"Can you take a break?" he asked.

"Can't this wait until later?" She needed a good twenty-four hours of sleep and some distance between them so she could forget about how those big muscled arms of his felt around her. But right now all she could see was him last night as he'd moved between her legs and made her his once again.

"It could," he said, moving slowly closer to the counter.

"Great," she said.

"I can come back when the shop is closed and take you to dinner," he offered.

She wanted to do that. Have a private dinner with him, but she knew she'd end up making love to him again. She needed to get out and do things with him that brought other people into their company. Otherwise, she'd fall back into bed with him and in two weeks he'd be gone and she'd be wondering why the hell she'd let him dominate her life again.

"I can't tonight," she said.

"Do you have plans?" he asked.

"Yes. I have a very busy life. You got lucky last night when you asked me to bring you that cupcake, which you never paid for," she said.

"Let me rectify that now," he said, taking out his credit card and handing it to her.

She went to the cash register and rang up his order from the night before and then slid the card through the credit-card machine. She focused on every detail of the mundane task, ignoring the spicy scent of his aftershave and the fact that he was so close she could reach out and touch him.

"I'll need your signature," she said as she tore the receipt from the machine.

She pushed the paper across the counter to him and handed him the pen with the flower on top of it that they kept in a jar by the register. His fingers brushed hers and a little electric tingle went up her arm.

How could one man's touch affect her so much?

"What are you doing tonight?" he asked.

"I'm going to meet friends at the beach after work. We're going to surf and do some paddleboarding."

"Sounds interesting," he said.

He was so close she could see the scar on the left side of his face more clearly. Last night when she'd been kissing him she'd concentrated on other places, but today in the bright sunlight that scar seemed more prominent.

"How did you get this?" she asked, reaching up to touch it.

"Our convoy was attacked. I went out looking for high ground to get a good shot, ran into an enemy combatant with a knife. We fought. He cut me."

The words were sparse but the image in her head was horrifying. She reached over and touched the scar again. She didn't know what to say. He stood there and let her touch his face. There was so much more to her ex-husband than she'd ever guessed.

"We're planning to have a bonfire on the beach tonight. Do you want to join us?"

He shook his head. "That's not what I had in mind. I wanted a private night with just you, me and not on the beach this time."

As empathetic as she felt toward him right now, she wasn't about to have another night alone with him. They needed to be with other people or they'd spend the entire time naked. And she'd learned more about Jay in the last five minutes than she had all of last night.

"My offer is the only one that's on the table at this time," she said.

"Fine, but I want to have a chance to talk to you properly," he said, handing her back the pen. "I need to get your opinion on a job offer I got today."

"Really? I thought you were just thinking about leaving the Marines," she said.

"I was. But near misses like this one," he said gesturing to his scar. "Make me think I might need to change professions."

"That's very true. But you've only been here one day… I didn't think you'd started job-hunting."

"Well, one of my buddies owns the company so it wasn't exactly hunting that had me find it. He knows I'm due to re-up and wanted to see if I'd be interested in joining him instead," Jay said.

She wasn't sure what any of this had to do with her but she did know it would be helpful for a long-term relationship if he got out of the Corps and took a job here. That was an interesting tidbit.

"What is the job?"

"Can you take a break? I don't want to talk about it in the store," he asked.

"Let me check with Staci," Alysse said. She left the shop to go into the kitchens and found Staci standing right inside the doorway, clearly eavesdropping.

"What are you doing?" Alysse asked her friend.

"Listening in on your conversation, obviously. So that's the guy?"

"Yes," Alysse said. "I guess you aren't working now."

"No. I hit a snag and need to think about what I want to do. I really want this dish to be more than a main. But it just tastes so bland… Not enough wow," Staci said.

"I'll give you a hand if you want," Alysse offered. Even though she knew Staci would decline the help. Staci was always trying to prove something to herself with her cooking, and, Alysse suspected, to the world.

"Nah, I'll figure it out. So are you going to do it, go talk to him?" Staci encouraged, peeking around the corner at him.

Alysse wanted to, but a part of her thought getting to know him better was stupid. He was the one man who'd hurt her worse than any other. Was she really going to open herself up to that kind of pain again?

"He is one hot-looking guy," Staci said.

"Yes, he is."

"I can see why you fell for him, but you aren't the same person you used to be. I think you are in the right place to deal with him," Staci said.

"Me, too," Alysse said with a confidence she was far from feeling. "I'll be back in twenty minutes or so."

"Take your time," Staci said. "It's not like we're busy right now."

Alysse took off her apron and went out front where Jay was still waiting. He was studying the glass cases but she sensed his attention was really on her.

"I'm ready to go," she told him.

"Good. Do you want to go someplace on my bike? Or we can walk," he suggested.

"Let's go to Old Town. It will be busy but there are a couple of quiet streets where we can walk and talk," Alysse said. Her plan to use Jay made sense when she was in the throes of wanting him sexually and trying to justify that to herself. Now, in the bright light of day, she wanted more. She wanted to find out what kind of man Jay was.

Finding out more about Jay would be hard and she'd have to stay focused because Jay didn't give up much information about himself and she didn't blame him because she also played her cards close to her chest.

She'd learned the hard way that being as open as she used to be didn't pay off. And she hated that she'd become so guarded and afraid to risk herself. Jay had stolen that confidence from her. She wanted it back, but she also wanted to fix him.

Oh, my God, she thought. That was what this was about. Jay was her latest project. Someone who needed her help. But she wouldn't fix Jay for herself. She'd help him so he could move on and so she could finally be over him.

JAY WATCHED ALYSSE out of the corner of his eye as they strolled down the hilly street. The weather was a temperate eighty degrees today and as he watched other people nearby he felt almost normal. For the first time in a long time he was exactly where he belonged, but he knew that was false. He didn't really belong with Alysse and even though to the world they probably looked like every other couple walking through town on this nice afternoon, he knew they were different.

She led him to a quiet park where an empty bench stood under the shade of a tall tree that he didn't know the name of. She sat down and stretched her legs out in front of her, then tipped her head slightly toward him.

"So, talk," she said.

She seemed relaxed, but in spite of her posture he could sense the tension in her. She wasn't sure of him and didn't trust him, and he knew that he would have to earn back her trust. He just wasn't sure he deserved it. Didn't even know how he'd go about winning her over because for years he'd been alone. And though he wasn't happy about it, there was a part of him that could get along just fine with Fantasy Alysse running through his mind.

It was safer that way. For him, certainly, and also for her. He didn't want to disappoint her again or hurt her anymore than he already had.

"Are you going to say anything?" she asked. "Or just keep staring at me?"

"I don't know how to begin. I've been thinking of the way you left last night. How you said you were going to use me."

"Maybe that wasn't the nicest thing to say," she admitted. She tucked a strand of her hair back toward the high ponytail it had escaped from and then rubbed her hands along her thighs.

"But that is who you are now. I made you into a woman who wants to use someone else. I did that," he said. He hadn't thought of anyone but himself when he'd left her in Vegas and he regretted that now.

He'd told himself he was doing it for her. That he wasn't the right guy to make her dreams come true. But he knew he'd left because he'd been unsure of what to do next.

She straightened up, twisting to face him. "I did that. Not you. I'm the one who put myself in a place where I can't find my way back to who I used to be. I'm not ever going to be that girl again."

She carefully put her hand on his wrist. "I need to do this and you're looking for answers, too. Don't worry too much. We'll do this together."

"I do worry. And I'm not someone who's ever anxious, but with you—I am. I am afraid I'm too hard for you. I already hurt the woman you used to be."

She bit her lower lip and he saw her hesitate and then she smiled over at him. "I've never complained about your hardness."

He chuckled. "I guess not. In fact, it probably works for your plan to use me for my body."

"It does," she said. "It definitely does."

"So where does that leave us?" he asked. Because, as he'd discovered last night, sex wasn't necessarily the answer to what he was searching for from her.

"It leaves us where we are. Two people who are

both trying to get who we are and where we're going, who enjoy sex."

"I need more than sex from you," Jay said. "You're different for me."

"You were for me, too, but then you became someone I didn't know. Let's try to start over."

"I don't know if we can," he said.

"We can. It won't be easy, but it will work. You told me you have a job offer…."

He pushed his sunglasses up on top of his head and turned to face her full-on. "I do. I'm not sure if it's the right thing for me or not."

"What is it exactly? I know we talked about you being a cake froster but I don't imagine you went out and found that kind of job opening."

He gave her a wry smile. "Your cookies are the only ones I'm interested in frosting."

She just shook her head and waited.

"It's a private security firm. They take on missions, some similar to what I've done in the Corps. They want me to be a sniper, which is what I've trained for and what I know."

"Sounds like what you're doing now, just that you'd be based here."

"Sort of. They aren't always deployed, so when they are here they do security for celebs… That sounds lame. Could you imagine me guarding some pretty face on the red carpet?" he asked.

She shook her head. "Definitely not. I'm sure they have stuff that's not that high-profile. Doesn't seem like sending you to a red-carpet event would suit your personality."

"Yeah, I'd have to ask about that. Lucien offered to let me try it out for the next few days until I have to re-up. That way I can see what they do."

She crossed those long legs of hers and swung her foot as she listened to him. Distracted, all he could think about was pulling her onto his lap, putting his hands around her waist and holding her close to him.

"I think you should give it a try. You said you were back here to see if there was something else for you—that you were at a crossroads. I can't imagine a job that would make your transition easier. I mean, you could try a government job, but I don't see you as a desk man."

"I'm definitely not a desk man."

"So, I guess that's settled," she said.

"Is it?" he asked.

"Isn't it?"

"Yes, it is. I want to give it a chance. But the crazy part is I don't even have a house. I always live in hotels when I'm on leave. If I do this it will mean a complete lifestyle change."

"You don't own a house?"

"I've never needed one," he said.

"What about an apartment?" she asked.

"No. I'm seldom in the States and when I am I use temporary quarters on base."

"Jay—no wonder the idea of being married to me sent you running. You've never had anything in your adult life like it," she said.

"I take it you own a home?"

"Yes. And a rental property with my brother," she

said. "Do you still want to come to the beach with me tonight?"

Hell, no. He had just established that he liked being apart from others and keeping himself removed, but he did want to spend more time with Alysse. So, he'd go to the beach tonight. Five years ago, it had been the thought of her big network of friends and family that had partially driven him to leave and this time…well, he guessed it was time to face them.

"Yes, I guess I do. But I don't have a surfboard or a wet suit. And I haven't surfed in over a year."

"No problem. I'll take care of that for you."

He walked her back to the bakery and then rode away on his motorcycle, pondering the fact that in the course of a few hours he had a job offer and a date with Alysse and her friends. He certainly wasn't in the Corps anymore.

ALYSSE HAD GIVEN Jay directions to the beach. It wasn't the one that the Marines stationed at Pendleton used. This one was farther up the coast near San Clemente, which was where she'd grown up. They were meeting Toby, her older brother, his girlfriend, Molly, Tommy and Jean, who'd gone to college with Toby, and Paulo and Frida, who they'd met at the beach about eight years ago and had started playing volleyball with.

Toby was a marine biologist as were Molly, Tommy and Jean. His true passion was the ocean and he spent as many hours on the water as he could. Tonight he'd spotted a new grouping of sea lions and they were all going to paddleboard out to look at them.

Paddleboarding consisted of standing on a board—

similar to a surfboard, and using a long pole to steer and move the board along. Alysse usually avoided going to these events even though Toby, who was two years older than she was, called her at least twice a week and invited her to do something with him and Molly.

And she usually went but lately she'd been busy at Sweet Dreams. Though it pained her to admit it, she was also a little jealous at Toby and Molly.

"'Bout time you showed up," Toby said, giving her a hug as she unloaded cookies from the back of her car.

"I'm early," she pointed out.

"I meant after putting me off for days. What made you change your mind tonight?" he asked as he grabbed her board from the roof of her car. She slung her beach bag over her shoulder and locked the car.

"I invited a guy to come along and join us," she said carefully. She hadn't realized that she was sort of setting Jay up by bringing him to meet her brother until she'd arrived here.

"Great. It's about time. So who is he?"

Toby knew about her marriage so she had a feeling that he'd be less than welcoming, which was why she'd come early.

"It's Jay."

"Your ex?"

"Yes. He's back in town."

"I don't like the sound of that," Toby said as they reached the beach area where he already had a small bonfire burning. He put her board down and turned to her with his hands on his hips. "Are you sure about this?"

"No, I'm not. But the bakery is a success now and I really don't know what to do next. I want to date, have a relationship, I thought, now I just don't know. I'm going to spend some time with Jay and see what happens."

Toby grimaced and stared out at the ocean. "God knows I don't have any advice for you on marriage, but I don't want to see you get hurt again."

"Me, neither," Jay said, joining them on the beach. "Sorry to interrupt."

She glanced past her brother at her lover. He wore a pair of khaki shorts and a Marine Corps T-shirt. He had those aviator sunglasses of his on and he looked every inch the tough badass that he could be. Toby glanced over at him.

"I've got my eye on you, Michener, and if you hurt Alysse again I promise you there is nowhere you will be able to hide from me."

"Good. That's how it should be," Jay said.

"Well, then…are you much of a surfer? I've brought a spare board you can use," Toby said.

"I've surfed a time or two." Jay stood taller than her brother and he had a more muscular build. For the first time in a long time she was seeing a man next to Toby who could hold his own. The few guys she'd brought surfing didn't really have what it took to cut it on the waves or with her brother. But Jay looked like he could.

"Great. You want to hit the waves with Alysse and I until everyone else gets here?"

Jay glanced over at her and she nodded. She and Toby had spent a lot of time surfing in their youth, waiting for waves and just talking quietly about whatever was happening with them. Their parents had divorced when they were four and two years old respectively, and their teenaged years had been interesting, to say the least.

"Love to. But I'm not really prepared, I don't have a wet suit," Jay said.

"I'll hook you up. Come with me," Toby offered.

Jay looked at her, and she said, "Go ahead. I'll change in my car and be right back."

"Sounds good," Toby said and led the way.

She admired Jay's backside and his muscled body as he followed Toby. She was definitely going to enjoy every moment she had with him because the last four years of her dating life had left her parched. And Jay was exactly the man to quench her thirst.

She grabbed her wet suit and then decided she'd just get changed right there on the beach. She should have put her bikini on before she drove up to meet Toby but she had wanted to get here before anyone else.

She donned her bikini under her sundress and then pulled on the bottom part of her wet suit. Most of the other people on the beach were doing the same thing. The families with young children had left for the day and the older crowd was coming out…well, young adults anyway.

"You ready?" Toby asked when he came back.

Jay was wearing the wet suit her dad used when he came to visit, and he had Toby's spare board tucked under his arm. He tossed his sunglasses in her bag and gave her a rakish smile.

"I like the way you look in that wet suit," Jay said, giving her a hot once-over with his dark chocolate gaze.

She blew him a kiss. "You look good, too, hot stuff."

Toby made a gagging sound, which was typical of her brother. Alysse laughed, thinking how perfect this moment was with her brother and Jay and the waves at their toes. She was so afraid to believe that things were good. And that worried her because with Jay she was always going to be waiting for him to leave.

7

JAY HAD SURFED off and on since he'd been stationed at Pendleton. Growing up on a ranch in North Texas he hadn't ever thought of surfing or the ocean much at all. Put him on a horse and point him toward some cattle and he felt at home.

But as he watched Alysse on her board catching the waves he was in awe. He caught a glimpse of how natural she was in this setting. This was a side to her he'd never seen before and he just sat back and lapped it up.

Toby had put on a friendly face in front of Alysse but in private had told Jay he was watching him. And Jay had to respect that.

He didn't have any friends or close confidantes that he'd mentioned his brief marriage to, but she had family—close family and friends. People she socialized with today who knew he'd married and left her.

Thinking on that made him wonder if he should just leave now. Alysse was way too good for the likes of him and the burden of being accepted by her friends was a high one. But then she paddled her board over toward him and sat up and smiled. Really smiled all the way to her soul, he imagined.

"Are you having fun?" she asked. The sun was behind her, casting her face in shadow, but he knew that she was enjoying herself. Her body language and easy laughter were all indications.

No, he wasn't having fun. But he did enjoy watching her enjoy herself and that made it worth it. He'd wiped out twice and even though it was just water swirling around him he felt as if he'd gone ten rounds with Lucien in a mixed-martial-arts match and gotten his ass handed to him.

"I'm a bit rusty," he said at last.

"Ah, that's not a big deal. Last summer we were slammed at the bakery, lots of weddings and special events, and I didn't get to surf once all summer. Come September Toby 'kidnapped' me from work and made me come out. I wiped out three times before I got out of my head. Maybe that's your problem…you seem to be weighing something very heavy."

He shrugged. There were a lot of positives about the Corps to him and one of them was that he didn't have to think about what to do next. If he reenlisted he'd have everything just the way it had always been.

If he didn't…he might have Alysse, a new job, a house… "There's a lot to think about."

"Of course there is. But this is a moment when you can let go and just for these few hours forget everything else and have fun with these people."

"There is only one person on this beach I'm interested in having fun with," he said.

"Me?" she asked, giving him a sultry look.

"Hell, yes," he admitted. "But you know that already, don't you?"

"I do," she said. "I am very interested in you, too, Jay but I don't want to make the same mistake I did before."

"It did sort of work for a while," he said.

"It didn't work at all. It was nice until reality started closing in. This time I want to know the real Jay. Who is the man with his clothes on?"

"And here I'd rather let you see me with my clothes off," he said.

"I like that, too, but today I learned that you don't own a home… That's huge."

"Is it?"

"Yes," she said, riding the swell of a wave that bobbed their boards. "It tells me you don't like roots."

He couldn't believe she was talking about this now. He wasn't prepared for it, but as natural as Alysse was on the water it probably felt like sitting around a kitchen table to her.

"That's true."

"What else don't I know about you?" she asked.

"You two going to take any waves or just keep talking like old women?" Toby called as he paddled over toward them.

Alysse called back, "We'll take a wave when we see one we like."

"Whatever," Toby said, paddling to catch the first in the next set that rolled under them.

"You should try to get to know some of the people in the group tonight. It's hard, believe me I know, but you'll enjoy it."

"Will I? Is that a guarantee?" he asked.

She leaned over and kissed him quickly on the lips. "Nope, but if you try it and it works, that's way better than the alternative. You taking this wave?"

He glanced back, thinking of what she'd said. He didn't have any answers and only knew what he wanted to happen but Alysse was right; he couldn't control any of that tonight. "I am."

He paddled toward the wave and his instincts and athletic ability kicked in.

The wave swelled behind him and he felt the board moving the way it was supposed to; he stood up and rode it. The sun was setting behind him and the beach seemed far away and there was no real noise around him except the sound of the water. This all felt so unreal. Not even a week ago he'd been up to his ass in desert sand without a drop of water in sight and now he was immersed in it. Alysse had been a memory; now he was with her, next to her, and who knows…

He tumbled off his board and was pulled into the water. The wave crashed over him and dragged his board; he felt the tug on his ankle strap. He held his breath and then swam to the surface watching out for his board so he didn't get conked on the head with it. He made his way to the beach and took off his ankle strap before picking up the board.

"You okay?" Toby asked from a distance.

Jay nodded and put the loaned board off to the side. There were other people there at the bonfire and they looked up at him with tentative smiles, but the conversation had ground to an abrupt halt as he'd approached.

Immediately, he turned away from the group and

began walking down the beach. He didn't belong in Alysse's life, did he need more evidence than what he'd just seen? This was a big part of her world and he was never going to fit in here.

He didn't understand its currents and patterns the way he did the corps. It didn't matter that he'd spent all his adult life in the Corps, he should be able to adapt to almost anything. What was the matter with him? Did he really not want to be with Alysse?

That was the answer he'd been searching for, and it'd been right here in front of him the entire time. He didn't fit in Alysse's life because he couldn't adapt the way she did. He'd seen her go from the bakery, where she was very at home, to the beach, and she probably had a dozen other roles she filled with ease.

He only had one. Marine. Did he want to leave the Corps behind and take a chance with Lucien and Company B? Or was he simply going to continue his same path? Honestly, he just wanted to stay where he was, but he knew that wasn't the way to a successful life, not anymore. Not for him, anyway.

"Jay?"

He turned and saw Alysse jogging toward him. She still wore her wet suit, which lovingly hugged every inch of her body. Her ginger hair appeared darker, almost brown, as it hung in long, wet tendrils around her face and his heart soared. He didn't want to leave her and yet he had no idea if he could stay.

There was no way he could ask her to be a part of his life while it was a mess. And tonight had proven beyond a shadow of a doubt that his life was really still FUBAR.

ALYSSE HAD THOUGHT TWICE about catching Jay, but in the end he'd looked so forlorn that she had no choice. He carried himself with pride. The man was an island and she felt acutely that he didn't want or need her or anyone else. But she couldn't just leave him to it.

Admittedly, she hated that she cared about Jay, because she shouldn't. He'd hurt her and she knew better than to trust him. But there was a part of her that understood the struggle he was going through.

"You okay?"

He clenched his jaw and she saw a glimpse of a man she'd never seen before in his eyes. He was a hard man and she had no doubt that he could survive in any dangerous situation he was dropped in, but seeing him now, like this, made her pause. He didn't know how to get along here.

She reached for his arm. He flinched away. She pulled her hand back and wrapped her arms around her waist, comforting herself. No matter what she projected on Jay, he was still a man whom she barely knew outside the bedroom. And though he'd never hurt her physically, he seemed to have an uncanny ability to find the right gesture to cut right through her.

"Of course I'm okay," he said, his tone terse.

"Whatever. So you're fine. If you don't want to talk to me I'm happy enough to just walk back. Is that what you want?" she asked. She was setting herself up here. It was a big gamble, giving him an ultimatum. But she had to try something. She hadn't even had a chance to introduce him to the others.

He didn't react and she started to return to her friends.

"No, wait. I don't want that."

She stopped and faced him. "What *do* you want?"

She wasn't sure what she'd expected tonight. Only knew that she needed to keep from being alone with Jay. But seeing him like this—uncomfortable and not himself—wasn't what she'd had in mind.

Even suggesting that he let himself forget about his troubles and just enjoy the waves hadn't helped for long. He wasn't like everyone else and she suspected that was part of the reason why she was so attracted to him. Yet that difference was something she didn't know how to bridge.

"I don't know," he admitted at long last.

"You're the only one who can actually fix that," she said. "Listen, I've got a short fuse where you're concerned so maybe I'm not the best one to be here with you right now."

He turned his head to the sea and she stepped closer to him, putting her arm around his waist because he seemed so alone. She wanted to comfort him. To take care of him, and she had a revelation that that was one of the very things that she'd always wanted to do for him.

"What do you want from me?" she asked.

"I don't know that either," he said. "Hell, I've gone from a man who had a career path he was sure of and a life that worked for him to this. I have no idea."

"That's okay," she said. "You're figuring it out. One thing I do know is that you can't keep hiding all the time. You need friends and you need to meet people who aren't in your line of work. Come back and eat with my friends. You *will* like them."

She tried to lead him back but he refused to budge. She sensed there was more to it than just being around strangers.

"What were you thinking on the waves?" she asked. "You were doing really well and then all of a sudden..."

"I wasn't thinking, like you said, and then I realized how ironic it was that I had been surrounded by sand not even a week ago and here I was on the water. It was just a surreal moment and I couldn't shake it. It got me thinking about going back and then I fell and you saw the rest."

"Wipeout," she said. "The water is a good place to think."

"Unless thinking makes you drown," he said.

She laughed because she thought that was what he intended her to do. But it was forced and she had some doubts that she was the right woman for Jay. For the first time she understood why he'd left her; her life was so different from his.

"I guess so. You're used to always being on edge. Maybe one of the other guys has a better surfing tip for you."

"I don't give a crap about surfing, Alysse. I'm not going to be out here all the time. I came here for you. I want—no, need—to be with you. That's all that really matters to me."

She wasn't sure how to respond to that. His words touched a place deep inside her that she was afraid to admit she still had. And she wanted him to really be here for her but she wasn't too sure he could be.

"I can't promise you anything. I'm seeing now how different we really both are," she said. She understood that her dreams of the future were bound to be very unlike his because he had never even had a home of his own. How could he possibly look at her and see plans for a distant future together?

"Why just now? What did you see that you didn't before?" he asked her.

"I thought we had some kind of common background, but I'm beginning to suspect we don't. I never asked you about your past. We never did the fifty-questions thing that most couples do when they first meet."

"Well, we sort of did, but the questions were more, do you like the way my mouth feels on your neck?" he said.

She shivered as a pulse of desire went through her. It would be easy to let this be about sex, but she refused to let it go that way right now.

"We both know I like it," she said.

"No, we never did the getting-to-know-you part, did we?"

"So…" she said, not about to let him divert her again. There was so much more happening with Jay right now than a bonfire on the beach. This was her chance to really get to know him and she wasn't about to pass it up.

"My family's from Texas, the northern part near the Oklahoma border. My dad had a ranch," he said, his voice taking on a reminiscent quality. "Our family had been ranching there for over a hundred and fifty years."

"Why aren't you a rancher?" she asked.

"We lost the ranch in my senior year of high school.

Had to move into town and live over the diner where I worked as a dishwasher."

"What kind of work was there for your dad?" she asked, trying to imagine how horrible it must have been to move during your senior year of high school.

"He took to the rodeo circuit taking care of the live-stock on the road," Jay said.

"At least you had your mom with you," she said. "That kind of change must have been hard."

"It was."

Silence grew between them and she realized that Jay wasn't going to offer anything else. Good thing she had a million questions.

"What did your mom do for a career?" she asked.

"She was a bank manager," Jay said.

"They make pretty good money, why did you have to live over the diner?" Alysse asked.

"Because she left us when I was eight. Had enough of the dusty, isolated ranch," Jay said. "Dad had to mortgage the ranch when she left and by the time I was in high school he'd fallen behind on the payments."

"That's horrible. Why didn't your mom take you with her?" Alysse asked. Jay's childhood had been so different from hers. Her dad had owned a car dealership and made good money. He and her mom had doted on both her and Toby and they'd had a fairly good life.

"Who knows? She always said I was a handful and more like my dad than like her," Jay responded.

"In what way?" she asked, trying to understand how a mom could leave behind her eight-year-old son. She tried to see the boy Jay must have been, but he was too much a man for that to happen. Any softness in him had been burned out long ago. He was a tough Marine through and through, and she saw the evidence with her own two eyes.

"Just rough, I guess. We hunted and took care of the ranch together. I was his little shadow. Everyone said so. I guess she thought I needed to be with him."

Alysse hugged Jay close to her, trying to comfort the little boy who had been abandoned. But she knew that she couldn't. That event had changed Jay. Could he ever trust, be with anyone?

She was beginning to wonder if she was fighting a losing battle where he was concerned. She knew she'd wanted to mend her broken heart but a part of her had hoped to find the keys to real happiness with Jay and she was beginning to believe that would never happen.

JAY LIKED THE FEEL of Alysse in his arms and knew that he was winning her over not by doing anything but simply by showing her parts of himself that he usually kept closed off. He hadn't wanted her to see the lost little boy he'd been, but he knew that this time he had to do things differently.

It occurred to him that they were finally alone. Exactly what he'd wanted all day. He pulled her closer, skimming his hands down her back until he could cup her buttocks. He wanted her.

He felt his cock stir and wished they were really alone. He scanned the area, hoping for an isolated place that would allow them to be all but invisible. He wanted to carry her away from here and make love to her and reinforce the bonds that were already there between them. His caring was the first step to winning her back.

"You okay?" she asked. "I didn't think I'd ever feel… sympathetic toward you, but all of that has changed. I want to know more about your past and more about the person you really are. Want to walk for a while and talk?"

No, he wanted to slowly strip the wet suit from her body and kiss her until they both forgot their names and where they were.

"I don't see why the past should have anything to do with you and me," he said.

"Well, maybe you left me before I left you…maybe the little boy you—"

"Stop. I don't think that has anything to do with it. I don't want to talk. I want to take you away from here and go someplace where we can make love and leave all the obvious differences behind us."

"You're running away again, Jay."

He knew he was. He'd probably always run away from her. She made him uncomfortable in his own skin, but at the same time he couldn't imagine not having her in his arms.

"I need more," she stated.

"I know that," he said. "Tell me about your upbringing. Where did you grow up?"

"Right here. Well, Oceanside, not San Clemente. My dad owned the local Chevy dealership and my mom did the books for him, even after they'd divorced. My brother and I got into the usual mischief but nothing too crazy. He went to UC Santa Barbara. I did one year at Berkeley before I flaked out and came home."

"Berkeley? You must be pretty smart," he said.

"Sort of. But I hated it. I came home and my dad

said I'm not supporting you if you aren't going to school and so I enrolled in cooking school. Found I really loved it."

"Looks like you ended up where you needed to be," he said. "What does your dad think of you now?"

"I imagine he'd be pretty proud of me," she said. "He died of a heart attack before I graduated cooking school. It was a huge shock for us. He went out jogging one morning and that was it."

"I'm sorry," Jay said. "My dad died on the road."

"How?"

"Drunk driver." He didn't like to think about that too much. It had happened during his first six months in the Corps and after that, Jay had nothing to come back home to.

"I'm sorry," she said.

For the first time ever, Jay didn't mind talking to someone about the past. There was something about Alysse that made some of the rougher parts of his life seem okay.

"Let's go back and join your friends," he said, taking her hand and leading her down the beach.

"Do they all know that we were married?" he asked, stopping before they got to the group. "I don't want to have to do the whole thing I did with your brother with each of them."

"Only Toby and his girlfriend, Molly, know," she said. "Don't worry, if this doesn't work out, we can go back to my using you for sex—but not tonight." She laughed.

"Why not tonight?"

"Because you'll leave and I'll stay here and paddle-board and pretend that I'm happy."

His gaze narrowed on her. "Why pretend?"

"Because I think you need something from me that has absolutely nothing to do with making up for the past. And no matter how hard I try to be objective, I just can't and that makes me just a little sad."

He swallowed hard, listening to the honesty that came so easily to Alysse and that made him feel small and ashamed. He wanted her, and he wanted his life to be so much easier than it could be right now. He was at a crossroads, she wasn't. So he could either be the man she needed him to be or he could move on.

"Fine, let's go back to your friends."

"Not like that," she said. "I didn't say that to force you."

"But you did. You're taking control of this relationship and I don't blame you. Just give me some time to adjust as we go along, okay?"

He saw her weighing it over and thought she might say no, and tonight, as aggravated as he felt at the world in general, he almost thought that it was okay if she said no. Major decisions could be influenced by things smaller than this moment. And if she said no now he would have no reason to stay.

"Sure, it's okay. This isn't easy for me either. I am still trying to find my way forward," she said.

He knew that and he understood that his coming back into her life had seemed to spur her on some sort of quest.

"Did you invite me tonight to see how much I didn't fit in or to get back at me?"

"No. I invited you because I thought it'd be nice for you to see what my life is like. To get a chance to know the people in my life and, as much as I want just to get over you, I also have a hard time not liking you."

"You are a paradox," he said.

"I'm not. I'm simple and straightforward. You just have to look beneath the surface," she said, leading him over to her friends—and he let her.

He wanted to go wherever she led him. Which was a sobering discovery because he'd thought he was back in San Diego to make a tough decision but more and more he was coming to realize he was back here because this was where Alysse was.

8

JAY HADN'T EXPECTED to be able to relax with the group at the bonfire, but one man stood up as soon as they arrived and greeted Alysse with a warm hug.

"How are you, *amiga?*"

"I'm good, Paulo," she replied. "I want you to meet Jay. Jay, this Paulo Ramones. Paulo, this is Jay Michener."

Jay shook the other man's hand. "It's good to meet you."

"You, as well," Paulo said. "This is my wife, Frida."

A lovely woman with dark hair and olive-colored skin walked over to them and shook his hand. "So nice to meet you."

Both Paulo and Frida had heavy Spanish accents and were fit and lean.

"The pleasure is mine," Jay said.

"This is Tommy and Jean. They both work with Toby. And this is Toby's girlfriend, Molly. She works with them, as well," Alysse said.

He waved at the group. "What do y'all do?"

"Marine biology. Currently, we're studying changes in migration habits of whales."

"Interesting," Jay said. "You, too, Paulo?"

"Nah. I play volleyball with Toby. We're on a competitive team in the Cal King tournament."

"Everyone ready for a veggie burger?" Toby asked.

The food was served and Jay found himself sitting on a large blanket with Alysse on one side and Paulo on the other. The group was all sitting fairly close together around the fire.

"Are you a baker like Alysse?" Paulo asked, after taking a huge bite out of his veggie burger.

Jay shook his head. "No, sir. I'm a Marine."

"Really?"

"Yes. Does that seem hard to believe?" Jay asked.

"No, it's just that I never thought a military man would be Alysse's type," he said.

"I guess I am," Jay said. Focusing on his plate.

"I meant nothing by that comment. I was in the special forces before we moved here. Have you been to Iraq?" Paulo asked.

"Yes," Jay answered, and saw the other man in a different light. They started talking about their respective deployments and places they'd been to. Paulo had gotten out and no longer did anything vaguely resembling what he had in the past.

"How do you like being out of the military?" Jay asked. He wanted to know how other people made the adjustment. It would give him some ideas on how he'd be able to do it if he decided to leave the Corps.

"I love it. But I went in because I'm the second son in my family and I was expected to have some military training. Though I play volleyball with Toby on the weekends, my real career is in wine. My family owns vineyards in Spain and here in California," Paulo said. "Is it like that for you?"

"I am just a military man," Jay answered. "Don't have anything waiting for me outside the Corps."

"I don't know about that," Paulo said, glancing around him toward Alysse who was having an animated conversation with Molly.

"It's complicated," Jay said. He didn't want to discuss his brief marriage to Alysse with a man he'd only just met. In fact, Jay knew he never wanted to discuss that one week in Vegas with anyone, ever. But he did like the thought that other people looked at him and Alysse and saw a couple.

The thought pleased him more than he'd expected it to. This night, while wildly different than any other he'd spent with her, was turning out to be really enjoyable.

"I'm not surprised. I liked the order of military life," Paulo said. "The discipline I learned there has helped me in my business. And I found that I liked stepping out of the traditional role my family had planned for me."

"Where is your vineyard?" Jay asked.

"Temecula. Have you been down there?"

"No. I pretty much stay near the base or go into San Diego," Jay said.

"You should take Alysse to Temecula and go up in a hot air balloon. You will get a nice view of the entire valley. If you do this, you call me and we will treat you to lunch at the vineyard."

"I will do that," Jay said, wondering if he could convince Alysse to take a balloon ride with him. He wasn't good at making romantic gestures and he wasn't even sure that she'd welcome them.

"Do what?" Alysse said.

"Bring you to my vineyard for lunch," Paulo said.

"That's a wonderful idea," Frida agreed, joining in the conversation.

"I guess that's decided then," Alysse said. "When?"

"We'll have to discuss the details later," Jay said feeling a wave of panic washing over him. He was still struggling to figure out him and Alysse. Adding more people to the mix right now might be too soon.

"Alysse has my number. You will call me, yes?" Paulo said.

"I will," Jay agreed.

Toby stood up and everyone finished up the last of the dinner and joined him. "Jay hasn't been paddle-boarding before so I'm going to give him a quick lesson. Anyone else need one?"

Frida raised her hand. "I'm afraid I've never done it before either."

"Follow me," Toby said.

Jay glanced back at Alysse and she just smiled at him. He knew he was making her happy by doing this and even though it was outside his own comfort zone, he followed her brother down to the water. He wasn't sure when it had happened but he'd come to realize that he'd do anything to see Alysse smile.

That was a dangerous thought.

She'd been important enough for him to come back

here and try again, but he hadn't understood how important until this very moment.

ALYSSE WASN'T SURPRISED when Jay followed her home from the beach. The evening had turned out differently than she'd anticipated. She'd thought that Jay wouldn't be so comfortable so quickly even once she'd introduced him. But after the initial hesitancy on his part, Jay had really made an effort. It hadn't been easy and luckily Paulo's military experience had made Jay feel right at home. But that had only underscored to Alysse the difference in the two men. Despite his time in the military Paulo was open and gregarious. He was affectionate and doted on Frida and seeing them together made Alysse long for something that she suspected she'd never have with Jay.

She was honest enough to admit that she knew that inviting him into her house and her bed tonight would be a mistake. But it had been a long day, full of ups and downs, and she wasn't ready to deny herself Jay. She had the feeling that he'd be gone soon enough. She wished she could be more like a movie heroine and just not worry about tomorrow, but she'd never been that way.

"You're taking a really long time to get out of your car," Jay said, walking over to her.

"I'm trying to decide if I should invite you in," she said, speaking honestly. Tonight had made her realize that she still wanted all of those dreams that she'd shoved aside when Jay had left her.

The only problem now was she wasn't sure if Jay was the man she wanted to have them with.

"I'd love that but I followed you because it's late and I couldn't live with myself if I didn't make sure you got in okay. Also, I wanted to know where you live," he said.

"Is it what you thought?" she asked.

"No. I expected you to live closer to Sweet Dreams," he said.

He seemed subdued and maybe a bit tired himself. He ran his hand through his hair, which had been flattened by his motorcycle helmet.

"It's late," he said.

"Yes, it is. I didn't sleep at all last night and I had to get up early. You'd think I'd be tired, but I'm not."

He opened the door of her car. "Come on, let's go inside."

"I haven't decided if you're coming in yet," she said.

"What can I do to make you invite me?" he asked.

"I'm not sure," she admitted.

"What if I said I'll hold you until you go to sleep?"

"I'm not sleepy," she said. "And you holding me will only make me long for things that I can't have. We both know that."

She exited her car and Jay closed the door behind her and stepped in front of her, so that she was trapped between his body and the vehicle.

"I don't know that holding you is a bad thing, Aly. I think you aren't sure either, otherwise you would have been out of your car and in the house like lightning. You want me."

"I do. Too much, but tonight just proved that a real relationship—"

He kissed her, stopping the words that were on the

tip of her tongue and she shivered as the one embrace she'd been longing for all day was finally here. She'd missed this—intimacy, but to be honest they'd never had it before. Though she didn't want to admit it, she'd missed Jay. In Vegas, life had been a pretty dream.

Noticing his hand in hers, she laced their fingers together and for a moment simply enjoyed the fact that she was coming home with her man. Something shifted inside her and she knew that nothing would ever be the same again if she brought him into her bed.

He slid his hands up and down her arms before they settled on her waist. She tipped her head back and let the magic wash over her. She forgot about all that her mind knew about Jay and let her heart lead the way, for tonight at least. She tunneled her fingers through his silky close-cropped hair and held him to her as her tongue moved against his. He lightly sucked on her tongue and she felt an answering response in her breasts as her nipples tightened. And lower in her most feminine area.

She wanted him—there was no denying it. Or herself, she thought. She was single and she wanted this man. She could have him.

He shifted his hips against her and she felt the tip of his erection nudging at her as the heat and passion swelled inside her. This was Jay—wounded warrior, sexy lover and the only man she'd never been able to forget. She wrapped her arms around him to hold him close. She had tried to pretend the emotions she felt for him were only lust, but she knew better. She couldn't lie to herself anymore. Jay's hand on her made her feel cherished and special to him. He tore his mouth from hers.

"Alysse…" He said her name on a long sigh and her heart skipped a beat.

"Do you want me?" he asked, whispering the question close to her ear.

"Yes," she said, surprised at the breathless quality of her own voice. She also wanted something that she was afraid to believe he could give her. She wanted his heart. "I've thought of nothing else since I saw you shirtless on the beach. You have a very tempting body, Jay."

"Then take me," he said.

She did want to take him, and yet at the same time learning about his past had made her afraid to really use him. Jay was more vulnerable than she'd realized. It was silly, because he seemed so strong and indestructible that it had never occurred to her he could be hurt.

"I will," she said. But she promised herself she would do her best to protect his heart, too. Because hurting Jay would only result in wounding herself.

She took his hand and led him up the lighted path of her small bungalow to the front door. She fumbled for her key and almost dropped it.

"Nervous?"

"Silly, huh?"

"Not so silly. We aren't strangers anymore."

That struck her. They'd married and divorced but hadn't really known each other. The impact of what she was doing held her still.

"I'll go," he offered.

If he left she'd never see him again—she knew it.

And she had to ask herself if she was going to hide away from life on the off chance that she might get hurt or if she was going to live it.

"No. Stay."

Jay smiled then, a real smile, and she felt that flood of emotion rushing through her again. He stooped, picked up her keys and handed them to her. She turned to put the key in the door lock and he came up behind her.

His hands were on her waist, his mouth on her neck dropping gentle kisses that stoked the flames of desire burning through her and convinced her she'd made the right decision in inviting him in.

She finally got the door open and they stepped into her foyer. Jay closed the door and leaned back against it. He stood there for a moment surveying her and her lovely house. He crossed his arms over his chest, his expression unreadable, and she wondered what he was thinking.

"Nice place," he said at last.

"Thanks."

There was awkwardness between them that hadn't been there before and she wondered if it was because in her mind this had all changed. She had admitted to herself how much she cared for him. There was no going back.

"Come here, Aly. Make me believe I fit in your world."

She took a step toward him and he pulled her into his arms. She held him closely, burying her head in his shoulder and inhaling his unique scent—the saltiness of the sea that clung to his clothes and hair, the earthiness that she always associated with Jay. He kissed her passionately and slowly, as if they had all the time in the world.

Then she felt him caressing her back, his hands roaming up and down her body, loosening buttons and zippers until they could slip underneath and touch her naked skin.

She shuddered. Oh, she'd missed his touch. She gasped as he spanned her waist with his hands and lifted her off the ground so that she was more fully pressed against him.

She pushed her hands under his shirt, rubbing his chest to tease him. Then he drew her closer still.

"Oh, Jay," she said, knowing her heart was in her voice.

He swallowed hard and she saw a brief hint of emotion flash in his eyes before he kissed her.

In an instant, their tender moment became one of white-hot lust. His mouth was on her neck, one hand on her breast and the other between her legs. She was shaking and on the edge of her climax in seconds.

His hand left her breast and she heard the sound of his zipper being lowered and then felt his hot cock between her legs. He turned her around, though she wanted to see his eyes, hold his face.

Behind her, he guided her hands to the door and then touched her intimately to test her readiness. She felt the tip of his cock and shifted backward to urge him inside. He'd aroused her; she wanted him, there was no doubt. And he didn't waste another second before he thrust inside her.

He tweaked her nipples and then reached lower to fondle her clit as his hips pumped faster and harder.

Blind desire consumed her.

But still the questions sped through her brain, still she wanted to see him.

Suddenly, she felt the intense contractions of her body as her orgasm began and his hands quickly went to her hips and to pull her into each of his thrusts. He sent her over the edge into a climax that made stars dance in front of her eyes.

He thrust once more, then twice again before his hot release came. Falling forward, he rested his head between her shoulder blades. She stood there until her breathing slowed and he slipped his arms around her waist and held her.

Eventually, he pulled away from her, but took her in his arms. "Bedroom?"

She put her hand on his jaw as she saw the haunted look in his eyes. For the first time she understood that he had no idea how to deal with the emotions she'd elicited in him.

She pointed down the hallway. She wanted to pretend she was just using him for sex, but when he came into her bedroom and lay down beside her, she knew it wasn't just sex. He might have been unable to face her when they'd made love earlier, but now he cradled her in his arms, cuddled her close and made her feel as if he wasn't ever going to let her go. She focused on his lightly hairy chest rising and falling until exhaustion claimed her and she fell asleep. It felt like a fantasy. She knew that this time with him wasn't real. She had to remember that, she thought, as she drifted off.

JAY DIDN'T SLEEP as he held Alysse in his arms, but he did enjoy having her naked body pressed to his side. She snored softly in her sleep and he couldn't for the life of him remember holding her this way in Vegas. If he had it hadn't been as important as it was now.

He knew he'd played into her thought tonight that she was using him for sex. She wasn't. No matter what Alysse told herself she didn't have it in her to use anyone, least of all someone she cared for.

He knew that if he were a better man he'd walk away. He wasn't exactly sure why he didn't, except that when he was with her, despite his indecision about the future, he felt okay.

He stroked her hair and glanced at his watch, knowing he should go. She had to get up early and she might not want him to spend the night.

But he was reluctant to leave. He didn't want her to wake up alone and think he'd abandoned her again. Damn, he was trapped. But it was the sweetest situation he'd ever found himself in. He felt his pulse slow and his eyes grew a bit heavier.

He rolled to his side, pulled her closer and drifted off to sleep. His dreams were dark and disturbing. He found himself back in Afghanistan, lying in cover, waiting for his target. He saw the dust rising in the east as a caravan of fast-moving SUVs headed toward him. He glanced at his scout and it was Alysse calling out the coordinates of the wind and the trajectory. And instead of lying down in cover she was standing next to him in her chef's jacket and hat.

What the hell was she doing here? Alysse should

never be in the battle zone. Damn. This was a huge mistake.

"Get down," he yelled. Rolling at her legs, knocking her to the ground so that she didn't present as large a target. She popped her head up and he pushed it down before tucking her underneath him. "It's dangerous."

"You were supposed to protect me," she spat.

"I'm trying," he said. But he knew they'd been spotted and heard the convoy stop below their position. She wasn't listening to his orders. She was putting them both in harm's way and he had no way to save her.

"Stop smothering me." She struggled against him and he felt the whiz of a bullet flying past his head. He grabbed her more firmly, keeping her in place underneath him.

"Stop moving or we'll die," he ordered. God, he couldn't let anything happen to her. He didn't want Alysse to die. He wanted her safe and happy.

He had to get her out of here. He wrapped his arms around her and scanned the area. He'd roll them down the hill to the safety of a small copse of trees.

"Jay?" she asked, her hand on his shoulder. "Wake up."

"What?" he asked. The dream faded away. He was in Alysse's bed, on top of her. She had her hands on his chest and lightly pushed against him. Dammit, he weighed at least a hundred pounds more than she did and he was crushing her.

"Sorry," he said, quickly rolling off her. He sat up and put his feet on the ground. With his head in his hands, he took several deep breaths.

"Are you okay?" she asked, gently touching his back.

"Yeah. I didn't mean to fall asleep," he said.

"That's okay. Do you want to talk about it?" she asked, pulling on a nightshirt and moving around to sit next to him on the edge of the bed. She wrapped one arm around his shoulders and he didn't want to let her comfort him. He'd scared her and jerked her out of sleep. He didn't deserve this, but he sopped it up. He needed her. And that was scary because as Alysse had said in the dream, he was supposed to be her protector and he had no idea if he could do that.

"Um…no, I don't want to talk about it," he said. Hell, the last thing he wanted was to relive a single second of that nightmare.

She glanced over at the clock and he saw that it was nearly 3:00 a.m. "I guess I should head out and let you go back to sleep."

"That's not necessary. I have to get up in about an hour anyway," she said.

He was still shaking a little and the effect of the dream was hard to dismiss. He had thought that he'd simply be able to waltz back into her life, answer a few questions for himself and then move on. But that wasn't the case.

"How about I cook for you?" she suggested. "I know it's early but we didn't really eat last night."

That sounded so normal and so comforting; she couldn't even know how normal and comforting. But he wasn't about to let himself stay here and put her in more danger. He knew there was no enemy waiting outside her door. The true enemy here was himself. He was a risk she didn't need to take. He finally understood why she'd wanted to use him and move on and he regretted that he'd thought he could change her mind.

She deserved a man who could hold her through the night and not wake her with nightmares, she deserved a man who could sit in her kitchen and watch her cook without feeling a need to escape. She deserved a better man than he was and he knew he had to leave now before she started to fall for him again.

JAY GOT UP AND PULLED ON his jeans and began to walk out but she was sitting on the edge of her bed, watching him, and he couldn't do it. He realized that this might have been why he'd left her when she'd been sleeping in Vegas.

"What are you thinking?"

"That I am a mess right now. I've never had a dream that real before. Not like that," he said, unable to stop himself.

"You aren't a mess," she said. "You're human. You're allowed to have cracks and to make mistakes."

He wanted to smile at her but didn't. Not now. But he'd always treasure this moment and recall it whenever he felt alone. He wanted to do something equally nice for her and decided he didn't have to run away after all. He could stay here for her until she left for work.

"So what are you going to show me how to cook?" he asked.

"I don't know," she said, getting to her feet.

She wore a nightshirt that said Kiss the Cook on it

and fell to just above her knees. Her hair was tousled and her eyes still a little sleepy but she looked good. The last thing he wanted to do was go and get something to eat. He undid the fly of his jeans that he'd just fastened and pushed them down his legs.

"What are you doing?"

"Taking you back to bed where we both belong," he replied, closing the gap between them and pushing her back onto the bed. He came down on top of her and her legs slid apart. His hips fitted nicely in the space there.

"We do seem to communicate better here than anywhere else," she said. "But I think you need to do something to get your mind off the dream you had."

"This is going to help. Believe me, making love to you doesn't leave room for other thoughts."

"Really? Why? Are you thinking about me?" she asked. She cupped his butt and arched her hips to rock.

"Like what?" she asked. "I'm thinking how right you feel between my legs. And how I like the feeling of your breath against my neck."

"I enjoy that, too," he said, reaching down to free his cock from his underwear and lift her nightshirt so that they were pressed, naked, together. It was easier for him this way.

"I also think about how pretty your breasts are under this shirt," he said, leaning down to rub his cheek over her breast until the nipple hardened. He leaned up and then put his hot wet mouth on her nipple, sucking her through the fabric of her shirt. Then he slipped the tip of his cock inside of her body.

"I love the way you feel when I first enter you, Aly.

When I'm not inside your body all I think about is when am I going to be able to make love to you again," he said, entering her slowly, inch by inch.

She pushed up, trying to rush him but he kept himself still. He wanted to drive them both crazy and make this last as long as he could. She shifted underneath him and then reached between his legs to cup him.

He moaned. "Oh, baby, that feels so nice."

"Good," she said, continuing to tease him. Then she bit lightly at the side of his neck and pleasure spread through his body. He felt his resolve weakening. He slipped another inch inside her until he finally gave up on going slow and took her, his entire cock filling her.

She shuddered and tightened her legs around his waist, lifting her hips. She groaned his name and he thrust again and again until he felt his orgasm about to wash over him. He reached between their bodies and found her clit. He rubbed it as he pressed into her again and this time her body contracted around his cock. She gripped his shoulders, and screamed his name, holding nothing back. Her release was complete.

He pumped into her once more before coming inside her. Seated, he lay there with his head resting against her breast, letting his breathing slow. He tried to shift to his side but she still had her legs around his waist and her arms around his shoulders.

"Don't go. Not yet," she said.

He moved sideways so that their bodies remained connected. The room felt cool now that the sweat on his body had dried, and though he knew he shouldn't stay, he ignored that voice. Instead, he pulled the comforter up from the end of the bed and tucked them both in it.

A part of him was more than ready to acknowledge that truly he didn't know how they might make a future together, but for tonight he was content to just hold her.

<u>9</u>

SATURDAY DAWNED BRIGHT and clear. It had been four days since the night at the beach and Jay had fallen into the habit of spending most evenings at Alysse's place. They'd taken his bike and gone for a long ride up the highway from San Clemente last night and while she hadn't been able to truly forget their situation, she had to admit she'd enjoyed it.

This morning, though, she really hadn't been able to think too much about Jay. The kitchen was busy with two additional bakers who were helping since she and Staci had an event.

Alysse and the part-timers finished loading the last of the cupcakes for the Dana Point anniversary party into the back of her van. She and Staci had hired the two college students for weekends primarily. Marissa and Courtney were both eager and followed orders well, and someday they hoped to have their own kitchens where they were in charge. Marissa had said as much to Alysse ten minutes ago when Alysse had made her redo the icing on one batch of the cupcakes.

Alysse had been hoping that with the bakery being

extra busy, she wouldn't be alone with Staci given what she and Jay had started...which was what? "Seeing each other" didn't sound right.

However, they had managed not only to see each other every day, but to spend their nights together, too. Still, there was no point to hiding; Alysse would be spending the next forty-five minutes alone in the delivery van with Staci.

She got behind the wheel and pointed the van north toward Highway 5 and the anniversary party. "Did you get your dish sorted?"

"Yeah, I think so."

"Good. Was it for something special?" Alysse asked, knowing she hadn't been paying that much attention to her friend's life lately as she'd been consumed with Jay.

"Actually, it is. I've decided to try out for *Premiere Chef,*" she said.

"Really? Isn't that a pretty intensive show?"

"Yes," Staci said. "It is. If I get on I'd be gone from Sweet Dreams for ten weeks. I wasn't sure how to bring this up because you've been busy with Jay and everything."

Was Staci thinking of leaving Sweet Dreams? Alysse didn't know if she could handle that right now. "It's fine."

"You look pale and about ready to wig out. It's just that I'm getting restless."

Alysse concentrated on her driving. "When will you know if you're a contestant or not?"

"I'm going to L.A. tomorrow to pre-audition. How lame is that? You have to try out to try out," Staci said. There was a note of nervousness in her friend's voice.

"Lame," Alysse agreed with a laugh, trying to act as if she was cool with it when inside she was slowly going into a meltdown. "Why are you doing the show? You don't have anything to prove."

Staci ran her hands through her spiky hair and then shook her head. "I do. I hate the thought of those cocky jerks on TV, whom I know I'm better than, being named Premiere Chef. I mean, come on," she said.

Alysse just had to laugh at her friend's ego. But she'd tasted Staci's dishes at more than one dinner party and knew that she had the cooking chops to back up what she said.

"You're definitely a good chef, but the competition on those shows is stiff and you've been a baker like me for the last four years," Alysse said. Baking was different than the type of cooking that Staci would be required to do on *Premiere Chef*. She'd have to cook a meal in less than ten minutes and come up with unique dishes under pressure. It was a challenging environment.

"I'm getting bored," Staci said. "I've wanted to talk to you about it for a while. The timing never seemed right."

"Talk about what?" Alysse asked. She hated this. Every time she started to feel comfortable and as if her life was on the right path, something like this happened. "Are you leaving Sweet Dreams?"

"I don't know yet. I want to do this competition to see if I still have it in me to run with the big dogs, you know?" she asked.

Honestly, no, Alysse didn't know. She liked the quietness of the bakery and the familiarity of the repeat customers. "I don't see it, although I can understand that you want more. You are Cordon Bleu–trained."

"Yes. And I think I'm finally ready."

"For this competition? Or is it about being on TV?" Alysse asked, trying to understand exactly what Staci wanted.

"The competition. I was working in a Michelin-starred restaurant in Paris before things went belly-up and I ran back here to the States. I want that again. Last night I dreamed I was on the line and we were doing forty covers. The kitchen was crazy and I felt the energy…I miss it."

"Then you have to go for it. You shouldn't deny yourself the chance to pursue your dream. After all, Sweet Dreams was my idea and you helped me get it off the ground," Alysse said. "So what do you need from me?"

"Just some time off to do the show if I get through the first audition. We should probably hire someone to help out with the baking," Staci said.

"Yes. We'll have to make some changes, I'd rather spend more time in the kitchen than up front so maybe hiring a full-time counter person would be better," Alysse suggested.

"That might work. Sorry to spring it on you like this, but you've been busy every night after work." Staci turned and looked out the window at the passing hills of Southern California.

"Yes, I have been," Alysse admitted. She'd been busy trying to avoid Staci and her asking about the bad-boy Marine she was dating, whereas Staci had wanted to tell her about this *Premiere Chef* thing.

"It's Jay that's making you rush out the door every night, right?" Staci asked.

"Yes, it is. We've been trying to get to know each other again," Alysse said. It seemed that she and Staci were both heading off in other directions. Maybe they'd both done as much as they could together and it was time for them to try things on their own again.

"And is that working?" Staci asked. "To be fair, you seem to be pretty happy most days."

Alysse shrugged. "I like him. He can be a challenge sometimes and I'm not at all sure that he's someone I can spend the rest of my life with, but going out every night reminds me of all I've missed. I guess, like you wanting to get back into a Michelin-starred kitchen, I had shut myself off from a lot of things."

"Yes, you had. As I have pointed out on more than one occasion. But I'm glad to hear you admit it. I've been worried about you for a while because the bakery can't be your life," Staci said.

Alysse hated to admit it but Staci was right. She'd let the bakery become her entire life, and, to be honest, she was still doing that. She gave Jay the few hours at night before she went to bed, and then she rushed out in the morning while he was still sleeping.

She was glad for Staci though. The more they talked the less panicked she felt about Staci leaving to pursue a different dream. She would get through this change the way she always did—by finding a new comfort zone. She could and would do it.

"I know. To be honest, I think I was hiding there. It took so much effort to get the place up and running but now we have it under control," Alysse said. And that was what bothered her. She liked the fact that she'd gotten the bakery to a point where things went smoothly. There was a lot to be said for having something in your life that did what it was supposed to.

"That's why it seems like I should audition," Staci said. Her friend was looking at her with a sort of question in her eyes.

"You are so right," Alysse said to reassure Staci, but she found that she'd kind of reassured herself, too. "We both need to stop hiding in Sweet Dreams and go after the things that pushed us to create it in the first place."

"True. It's funny that we both were able to make something so successful and safe out of our disappointments," Staci said.

It was, and it spoke to the women they both were, Alysse thought. She and Staci had run away from their problems by going into the kitchen and creating something new. Something that no one else had any control over and Alysse realized that sharing Sweet Dreams with Staci had helped her to survive that first year after Jay had left.

"I've never said it, but thank you for being my partner," Alysse said. Staci had given her something other than winning to focus on. Without her dad or Toby in her life Alysse knew she'd have been moorless, just drifting from competition to competition, even though her mom had warned her she'd burn out.

"We're da bomb. I'm not leaving the partnership, just the day-to-day stuff," Staci said. "We've got a good thing going."

"Yes, we do," she said.

Alysse pulled into the parking lot at the Dana Point

Marina and drove toward the center area near the yacht club so she could park the van for unloading. And, as they set up their cupcakes under the tent prepared for them, Alysse realized that she had wanted life to be predictable and safe but it never was. Even while she and Staci had been hiding at Sweet Dreams their pasts were waiting there to spring up again.

She was very glad that she was ready for the change. She had to stop hiding from the truth about Jay. The truth was hard to face but as she stood in the late-afternoon sun she admitted to herself that she still cared for Jay and the last thing she wanted was for him to walk out on her again.

They'd been playing house together, careful not to talk about anything of real importance. He didn't discuss Company B with her any more than the one time she'd asked about it and he'd answered with a simple yes or no. So she'd stopped asking. She knew that they both needed to face some hard truths about their life together.

Now Alysse was thinking that Staci's bold move meant that it was past time for her to step up and make some changes. She couldn't just keep bumping along, because sooner or later she and Jay would have to talk about what they both wanted.

She knew she wanted more than what they had but she was afraid to admit it in case that would drive Jay away. By not admitting it, she wasn't going to have what she really wanted anyway.

JAY WAS STILL UNEASY about working out of an office, but Lucien had paired him with Donovan O'Malley on a basic mission where they would be guarding a foreign dignitary. It was right up Jay's alley, which was good because he found himself thinking about Alysse at the most inopportune times.

"What branch you with?" Donovan asked. He was about Jay's age and from Seattle.

"Corps. You?" Jay asked as he studied the other man from behind his aviator shades. The man was shorter than Jay and had more muscles. He had a buzz cut and a tribal-armband tattoo down his left arm. He wore jeans and a T-shirt and had done a good job of blending in with the crowd, even though Lucien had told Jay that Donovan didn't have any special recon training.

"Army. I'm an infantryman, what about you?" he asked.

"Sniper," Jay said. They had snipers in all the branches but he'd been trained by the best in the world, in Jay's humble opinion.

"Have you been to Afghanistan?" Donovan asked. "I did two tours myself, but I got a bit tired of all that sand. I'm used to lots of lush greenery and rain."

"I've been twice. I hear you on the sand. It gets in everything."

"Yeah. That's why I thought this job would be nice," Donovan said, scratching the back of his head. "I was tired of dusting dirt off my cot before I went to bed."

"Me, too," Jay admitted, although he hadn't slept any better the last four nights in Alysse's comfortable sand-free bed. That had nothing to do with the mattress or the sheets and everything to do with Alysse. He'd been afraid to sleep in case he had another nightmare.

"So what do I need to do next?" Donovan asked. "I

don't want to screw this up. And I've never done anything like it before."

"You won't screw it up. You any good with a camera?" Jay asked, pulling a Nikon from his backpack and holding it out.

"I'm fair enough. What do you need shots of?" Donovan asked, taking the camera from Jay.

"The entire building and all the entrances. Do it close up from the sidewalk and then walk across the street and get some there. I'm going to check out the buildings nearby."

Donovan nodded and started to walk away. "No problem. I'll meet you back in thirty."

"Sounds good," Jay said, but the other man was already gone. Donovan was very good at taking orders—the kind of man who would be an asset to any team he was on.

Jay liked to get the lay of the land by walking it. He'd done it a thousand times before with a scout at his side.

He made notes and sketched a few things. They were in Santa Monica and close enough to the ocean that the breeze would make anyone targeting the guy Lucien was guarding difficult to shoot. It wasn't an impossible shot, but most guys wouldn't be able to hit their target with one bullet.

He sat where he'd sit if he were assigned to take out the target and made notes of the wind direction and the patterns as it changed. And, though he knew it was impossible, he could swear the ocean breeze carried the scent of Alysse on it.

Damn, he had no idea what he was going to do with

that woman. He was no closer to figuring out his future than he had been when he'd ordered that special cupcake from her.

This job wasn't the solution to the restlessness inside him and he was coming to realize that Alysse wasn't either. It was as if he'd lost a part of himself when he'd been alone in the hospital recovering. He reached down and rubbed the top of his thigh where he'd had the injury. It didn't hurt but he continued to remember the sensation.

Maybe he'd been meant to die and being here now... that was the mistake. He'd seen men with a hell of a lot more to lose than him die over there and that had bothered him. Why had he been spared when no one would have mourned for him? When men who had wives and kids back home hadn't made it out?

There were some questions that were too hard to answer and Jay pushed them aside as he always did. For whatever reason, he was glad he was here now and that he had a second chance with Alysse. Maybe that was why he'd been spared?

His phone vibrated and he saw that it was a text message from Alysse.

Do you have plans for dinner? How does a sunset cruise from Dana Point sound?

I'm still working and won't have an idea when I'll be finished for another thirty minutes.

Okay. Text me when you know.

He finished his recon and met back up with Donovan. They'd driven up to L.A. separately so meeting Alysse wasn't going to be an issue of transportation, but he was feeling as though they were doing Vegas all over again, not really being themselves. A part of him enjoyed being with her, but he knew that wasn't going to be enough for her. And every day they were together he felt further and further away from her.

"Are the photos okay?" Donovan asked.

Jay took the camera from the other man and, using the small view window, scrolled through them. They were actually pretty good. There were one or two that showed some areas Jay thought might pose a problem.

"How was the visibility of this alcove?" Jay asked, pointing to an entryway on the side of the building that was covered.

"Not the best, but there is only one shadowy area and it's not big enough to hide a man."

"Are you sure?" Jay asked. The mission to protect the dignitary had been assigned to him, but the intel was going to be his. He wanted to give Lucien the best information he could. Make sure his friend didn't get caught out by anything that Jay or Donovan overlooked.

"I'm sure. I watched it for about ten minutes and there was a lot of traffic in and out. No one just appeared. There's a guard there, as well," Donovan said.

"Good to know," Jay said.

They finished chatting and then headed back to Oceanside and the Company B offices. Jay texted Alysse he was busier than he'd thought he'd be and that he'd get in touch when he was done.

She didn't text back. That silence made him wonder if he'd done the wrong thing and finally put her off. He pushed it to the back of his mind as he entered the conference room and sat down at the table with the rest of the team. Lucien was at the head of the table with Donovan and Jay next to him on the left. Across from them were two men whom Jay didn't know but he quickly learned they were both assigned to guard the dignitary.

The client was a foreign minister from Egypt who'd managed to escape the country before being arrested and was applying for diplomatic immunity.

After they reported on what they'd found in Santa Monica, Jay and Donovan both were done for the day and left the conference room. But Jay felt restless. He wanted to stay and offer his services as eyes in the sky. He knew that those two guards would do their job, but he felt that he could benefit the mission.

The only problem with that was that he didn't work for them. Today had been challenging and the kind of work he liked to do, but yesterday he'd sat in a control room and monitored security cameras, which had been a total bore.

He pulled his phone out of his pocket and saw that Alysse had texted him back that she was staying for dinner and if he decided to show up he could join her.

ALYSSE HAD ALWAYS STRUGGLED with being alone in public. Partly it was because she'd always felt so self-conscious that being alone made her feel exposed. But after Jay had left and she'd spent all those nights alone having to rebuild her confidence, something had changed. Her mom often said that it was as if part of Alysse stopped caring what other people thought. And Alysse didn't know if that was true, but she had finally stopped building her life around the romantic fantasy that had always existed in her head.

She was having a drink at one of the many bars in the marina area and sitting outside where she had a nice view of the Pacific. Staci had unexpectedly met up with one of her former boyfriends and gone with him when they'd finished the cupcake giveaway, and, instead of heading back to the bakery and her home, Alysse had decided to stay here.

She had a lot to think about, what with Staci wanting to go off and do her own thing. And Jay.

He'd been so accommodating a part of her had just expected him to say yes when she'd asked him to meet her, but then she guessed it was important to remember that he was busy away from her.

She took another sip of her wine and leaned back in the chair. The marina was busy with foot traffic—couples and families taking a stroll. In the distance she heard the sound of a reggae band playing. The marina committee had a full schedule of events that were going until late tonight.

She stretched and turned to signal her waiter and was surprised to see Jay approaching. He wore his habitual jeans and a T-shirt with a thick leather bomber jacket over it.

He pulled out the chair next to her and sat down. "Sorry I couldn't get here sooner."

"I didn't think you were coming," she said at last,

realizing that she hadn't gotten over her expectation that he would leave her.

"I wasn't sure I would either," he said. "The traffic from L.A. was nuts. I don't know how people drive here all the time."

"This job is demanding?" she asked. "You haven't said much."

He hadn't shared a lot of his life with her. In fact, if it wasn't something she pulled out of him, he never volunteered information about himself. She suspected he was just used to playing his cards close to his chest.

"Today I went and did recon for a job they're doing tomorrow. Guarding a dignitary at a dinner. I was checking out possible places where a shooter could set up in case…well, the guy's a target so there is no in case."

She heard some excitement in his voice as he talked about it. He ordered a beer from the waiter and then stretched his long legs out and looked over at her.

"Do you think you will take the job?" she asked. "It definitely sounds like your kind of thing."

"Today was. But other jobs they have aren't as interesting," he said, taking a swallow of his beer. "I don't know yet."

He wasn't going to make a decision that quickly and even if he did it would have no impact on her. Had things between them changed at all in the week they'd spent together?

She knew they had an electric sexual chemistry and she had to admit he'd let her use him for all the sex she wanted. But the truth was the more that she was with him, the more she wanted him. He wasn't curing her so she could move on. She was falling for him and that loner persona of his, even though she was trying not to.

"Would you like it if I took that job?"

"I don't think that's up to me," she said. "I don't want you to hold it against me if I say yes and you hate it."

"That's fair enough. Have you thought about us in the long term?" he asked.

She shook her head. "No. Have you?"

He didn't say anything, just took a long draw on his beer and she honestly had no idea what that meant. It occurred to her that while she'd been busy trying to cure herself of Jay, he'd been doing his best to protect himself, too. Maybe they just weren't meant to be together.

"What are you thinking?" he asked her.

"Nothing," she said. No way was she spilling her guts to him. He couldn't even talk to her about the simplest of things. Wouldn't give her an answer about anything connected with the two of them.

He shook his head. "You look sad."

"I'm not. I'm concerned about the bakery," she said. "That's probably what you're seeing."

"Why concerned? I thought everything was going well there," he said.

"It is. But Staci told me today that she wants to take a more backseat role in the day-to-day running of the store. It's going to be a big change," Alysse said.

"You can do it. What will be the biggest obstacle?" he asked.

She had been toying with that. "I think finding another baker. Most of the really good ones already have permanent jobs and it's so personal in the kitchen I need to find someone who suits my style."

"If it was me, I'd make a list," he said. Reaching into his pocket he pulled out a pen and a small notebook.

"Jot down the qualities you are looking for and then you can draft an ad or ask around to see if someone who matches them is available," he said.

She smiled at him because for the first time today she didn't feel alone. She hadn't anticipated that Jay would be able to give her this. She needed to feel as though she had a partner when she had these kinds of decisions to make. And frankly, given the way their relationship had been going, she hadn't had a clue that he'd step up to the plate this time.

She couldn't help staring at him and seeing some changes that made her care just a little bit more for him. Jay was the kind of man she could count on in a crisis and that shouldn't have surprised her because of his experience in the Corps.

For the first time she thought about Jay as someone who lived life on the edge, as someone who protected those he cared for. Yet she wasn't entirely sure he was going to be able to watch over her for any longer than his leave.

10

JAY WAS nervous.

He'd agreed to go with Alysse to the volleyball tournament and watch Toby play, which was no big deal, except that he'd also be meeting her mother.

"Ready for today?" Alysse asked as she and Jay headed for her car. The Saab convertible was perfect for the sunny California weather.

"I guess so. Why wouldn't I be?" he asked.

"My mom is coming today," she said. "I didn't mention it before because I didn't think anything of it until Staci texted me this morning that she was looking forward to the fireworks."

Great. "I guess your mom will be like your brother then?"

"What does that mean?" she asked.

"That she'll be angry with me," he said.

"Well, yes. That's her in a nutshell. She's very protective of my brother and me. When we were in school we could never let her know if someone teased us on the playground or gave us a hard time after school…

she'd head right into the principal's office and defend us."

"Sounds perfect to me," Jay said.

"I can see how you would think so given how your mom was," Alysse said. "But it was embarrassing."

"I get that. I...how should I handle her?" he asked. He wasn't too happy with the way that Alysse mentioned his past with his mom as if it was normal and okay. But her acceptance of it and of him made things easier on him.

"Just be yourself. Once she sees that you weren't out to hurt me she'll ease up," Alysse said, holding the key ring up and dangling it from one finger. "Do you want to drive?"

"Yes," he said. "You are a speed demon in this car."

She chuckled. "It's not my fault that it has really good pickup."

"No, but it is your fault that you like going fast," he teased, giving her a quick buss on the lips before opening her door. She slid into the passenger seat and he went around to the driver's side.

He was trying to behave normally, as if this was going to be fun, while truthfully, he was dreading it. Over the last week they'd done more things with her friends than he would have thought himself capable of. He'd chipped away at his defenses and, frankly, he believed it was making a difference.

"What exactly is the Cal King Tournament?" he asked once they got on the road.

"It's a series of semi-pro beach volleyball games. Toby and Paulo are on a team. Each team has two people and they play all day. There is a final at night.

The matches can be really competitive and a lot of fun to watch."

He wasn't convinced that going to an event that had all of Alysse's family at it was going to be fun. But he'd agreed mainly because he was test-driving normal life. He'd been working every day for the last week at Company B and spending most of his nights at Alysse's house.

There was a certain comfort to the days but every night he woke in a cold sweat. Since that first night when he'd woken Alysse up, he'd managed to get out of bed and leave her sleeping.

Today was a Sunday and the bakery was closed and Jay was helping Alysse cater for her family at the volleyball tournament. He wasn't looking forward to meeting Alysse's mom given the way Toby had reacted toward him, but he wasn't a coward and would do his best for Alysse.

"Thanks for coming today," she said as they started unloading the trunk of her car.

"No problem," he said, watching as she stacked items on her cooler with wheels. He was impressed at how well they all fit on there until he realized that she normally had to carry everything herself and she'd devised this method to move stuff quickly.

He felt ashamed at that. But set it aside. He was here now and he wanted to make up for the past, but that wasn't enough. He'd realized that at Dana Point. She did need a man who was there. Not someone who was off fighting in a war halfway around the world. So, he factored into his decision that if he wanted a future with Alysse he couldn't go back into the Corps.

She started to tow the cooler with all the stuff and he stepped around her, brushing her hand away and taking over control of the contraption.

The sun was warm and the crowds were heavy when they got to the beach. Alysse took her cell phone out of her pocket.

"I'm going to text my mom. She's been here since six saving a spot for us," she said.

"That's early."

"Well, she's all about family events. She'd have gotten here at midnight if she'd had to," Alysse said with a laugh.

Her phone vibrated and a minute later Alysse led the way to a large easy-up with a bamboo mat and a table under it. The woman waiting for them was tall and resembled Alysse. The two women hugged and Jay stood to the side.

"Mom, this is Jay. Jay, this is Candi, my mom."

"Jay," she said, holding out her hand. She wasn't friendly and didn't really smile at him, but that didn't bother Jay. He expected that Alysse's family would treat him coldly until he could prove that he had changed and wasn't back in her life to hurt her all over again.

"Ma'am. Where do you want the food?" he asked Alysse.

She motioned to the table and he started unpacking stuff. He supposed if he were a different guy he would have made some kind of small talk, but that wasn't his style and he knew it would sound forced if he attempted it.

He stayed to the side and watched as more of

Alysse's family arrived. They were all chattering away and he felt like an outsider.

"Hey," Alysse said, slipping up beside him. She wrapped her arm around his waist and he almost hugged her back but felt as if too many people were watching them.

"You okay?" she asked.

"Yes. Just a little outside of my comfort zone. When does the volleyball tournament start?" he asked.

She dropped her arm and stepped away from him. He felt like a cad but he thought it would be better if there were no public displays of affection while her mom was standing nearby with a disapproving look on her face.

"It's already begun," she said. "What's up with the cold shoulder?"

"Your mom looks like she's just waiting for an excuse to lay into me. And I don't think you'd appreciate a scene with your family and friends here."

"I wouldn't, but then I don't think she'd cause a scene," Alysse said. "What's this really about?"

"I'm not comfortable in crowds," he said. "There are too many people here. I can't relax like this."

"You did okay the other night when we went surfing with everyone," she reminded him.

"The beach wasn't this crowded," Jay said.

It was a hard situation to handle when there were this many people around. It wasn't just the strangers on the beach; it was Alysse's people under this tent. They were her community, her lifeblood and if he needed any proof that he and Alysse didn't belong together, well, here it was.

Alysse enjoyed this crowd and eating and talking and holding the babies and playing with the younger kids. And all he wanted to do was find a place with a wall that he could have at his back. They were so different and yet he was coming to need that smile of hers and her calming presence in his life.

"I didn't realize the crowds would make you edgy," she said. "Maybe after you've been out of the Marines for a while that will change."

He stiffened. He wasn't sure he'd ever lose his edge. "Maybe. You know I haven't made a decision yet on the Corps."

She gave him one of those odd searching looks of hers and he wished he understood what she meant by it. He hoped that she found the answer she wanted in his face. But when she sighed and turned away, he knew she hadn't.

"I know."

"Sorry," he said.

"It's fine. I need to remember that you aren't really here to stay," she said, shaking her head. "I think we've both been deluding ourselves that we were exploring options but really we've been playing house. And that's not all that different from what we did in Vegas."

"You're right. Here's not the time or place," he said.

"Agreed. I think Staci's just arrived and I'd like to have one day where I can pretend I'm like every other woman my age," she said.

"What do you mean?"

"You know, that I have a boyfriend and my family and friends are with me," she said before striding away.

He wasn't sure how he'd done it but he knew he'd just hurt Alysse again.

ALYSSE WANTED TO IGNORE Jay but that was exactly what she suspected he wanted her to do. He needed the silence and liked his solitary life. Why was she trying so hard to make him into something he wasn't?

And she *was* trying. She could have just stuck to her original plan and had sex with him every night until he went back to the Marines, but no, she had to have dreams and want more from him.

She was coming to believe that there was no way to cure herself of Jay and find another man, because, in reality, she only wanted him. That fact made her want to cry or scream or maybe punch Jay really hard.

But it was hardly his fault that he couldn't be what she needed him to be. If she'd been a different kind of woman she could have taken him as he was and been content, but she wasn't.

She wanted him to blend with her family and to fit in with her friends. Instead, he sat in a lawn chair drinking a beer, watching the game. She was mad at herself because all the growth she'd thought she'd achieved during the last four years was really nothing at all. She'd been fooling herself.

"Why are you glaring at the potato salad?" Staci asked coming up behind her. "I've tasted it and it's good."

She gave her friend a half smile. "No reason. Just not sure if I should put an ice pack underneath it."

Liar, she thought. Why didn't she ever really talk to her friends about her problems? She was just like Jay in that—she had to sort it out herself. Maybe that was part of the reason she was so attracted to him.

"Well, considering you've already got two under

there I'd say no," Staci said. Her friend took her arm and turned her toward her. "What's up?"

Alysse shrugged and fiddled with her sunglasses. She'd been pretending that she and Jay could have a normal life together but this afternoon was just showing her how wrong she'd been. They were different. Not just in little ways but in huge ones. And... "I guess I'm just facing reality."

"Ha. You are the most grounded person I know," Staci said, tapping her on the forehead. "You overthink everything. Is that what you're doing now?"

"Not really. I'm still clinging to a few girlish fantasies that I should have gotten rid of a long time ago," Alysse said. She didn't want to admit that she'd been hoping that Jay would completely change and become the kind of man that would suit her life the way it was. That wasn't Jay. He did his own thing. He had his own strengths and those were what had drawn her to him. But those strengths were also his weaknesses.

"I'm guessing this has something to do with your Marine," Staci said in her wry tone.

"It has everything to do with him," Alysse said, wishing that for once her romantic life would be easy. But it never had been. Even in high school she had struggled with dating. Her mom had said that once Alysse was an adult she'd understand what she really wanted from a man but she still hadn't. "I can't figure him out."

Staci threw her head back and laughed. "You are kidding me, right? Men are from another planet. You will never be able to understand why he does whatever it is that is upsetting you."

Alysse smiled, then felt just a tad melancholy think-ing about Staci being up in Los Angeles while she was in San Diego. It was only about a three-hour drive but it would seem a world apart.

"I guess you are right. You know, I'm going to miss you when you're in L.A."

Staci hugged her. "I know. But don't sweat it. I'll be coming back to visit. And if I get kicked off the show early, I'll be back for good."

"I thought you wanted to try something new?" Alysse asked her. She was afraid that she was project-ing her vulnerability at the thought of losing her best friend and Jay within a few weeks of each other. And it was beginning to seem more and more that no mat-ter what career path Jay took he'd more than likely not be with her. Different people, different paths.

"I do, but that's not fair to you. You have to find a new baker and new staff for the front of the shop," Staci said.

A lot was changing all at once and Alysse had been sort of ignoring it to deal with Jay. But she knew that she couldn't let the rest of life fall away because of him.

"I can handle it. It's not that big a deal. And I don't want you giving up just because you're worried about me. I'm way stronger than I look," she said.

That was when she realized that she was putting Jay through a test to see if he'd sacrifice what he wanted for her. Why was she doing that? It was as if she was afraid to trust him.

Hell, she *was* afraid of that very thing and had been since she'd stepped onto the beach at the Hotel Del Coronado and found Jay waiting, instead of some stranger. And she knew that no matter what she did or said, she was never going to be able to treat him like some guy she'd just met.

They would always have their past and she wasn't able to let that go. She was trying to make him be a part of a life that she wasn't too sure he'd ever be able to accept. Why?

Because it would be safer for her. If Jay wanted the same things she did, then he wouldn't leave her and she'd be able to let her guard down around him. Instead, since she was treating him with kid gloves, he was edgy and so was she.

"You should go for it, Staci. Don't feel like you have to come back to Sweet Dreams. If you want to though, your station in the kitchen will be waiting for you," she assured herself and her friend.

"Thanks," Staci said. "It'll help me out, knowing you've got my back. I think that we can invite friends to attend some of the cook-offs. Would you come?"

"Hell to the yeah," Alysse said, being silly because now that she'd figured out what she was doing to herself and Jay, everything seemed a little brighter.

"I'll be right back," Alysse said.

She left the table area and headed over to Jay. It was one thing to realize they'd been playing house but another thing entirely when she admitted that she'd set it up to test him. Did she honestly think that if they lived together and had these pretend lives together, he wouldn't leave?

She knew that she had been playing games with herself and trying to entice him to stay by showing him her family and friends. Today she had got it—if she wasn't enough for him then all the cool people she surrounded herself with wouldn't make her satisfy him either.

Jay was searching for something and she couldn't give it to him. If he could fulfill that part of himself that had been missing with her, then maybe they had a chance. And if he couldn't, it was time for her to cut her losses and move on.

Alysse couldn't find Jay at first and then noticed her mom was missing, too. She scanned the beach and found her lover standing in the shade with a brick retaining wall at his back. She smiled at that, but the smile soon left her face as she spotted her mom standing next to Jay and talking very animatedly to him.

Jay was nodding and had his arms crossed over his chest. He was being respectful or at least it seemed that way to her from where she was. And she felt a moment's panic. What if this scared him into leaving her again?

She took a deep breath and then let it out.

There it was, she thought. The fear that dominated every second of her thoughts and lurked in the back of her mind. She hated that she was filled with fear, but even acknowledging it wouldn't make it go away.

The only thing that would was some reassurance from Jay and she knew that was asking the impossible. She walked briskly over to her mom and Jay and they stopped talking when they saw her.

"Am I interrupting?" Alysse asked.

"No," her mom said. "I was just telling Jay that I haven't seen you this happy in a long time."

Really? Then she looked at Jay and he was grinning. He'd enjoyed chatting with her mom about her. She didn't know how he'd done it but they both seemed to be getting along. "Well, I am happy right now."

"Good. I warned Jay that if he made you cry again I'd come after him and I might not have his skills with a weapon but I do know how to protect my own," her mom said.

"Candi, I can respect that," Jay said.

"Good," her mom said. She patted Jay on the shoulder. "Thanks for listening to me."

"No problem," Jay said. Her mom gave Alysse a quick hug and then returned to the picnic area.

"What was that about?"

"She had some things to say to me and needed to clear the air," Jay replied.

"Was it okay? Did she upset you?" Alysse asked.

"I'm a man, Aly, I don't get upset," he said.

"Then what do you get?" she asked.

"Pissed off. But your mom really loves you and only wants what is best for you, and I can't get mad about that," he said.

"Good. I wanted…I'm not sure how to say this," she said. Now that she was standing in front of him the words she wanted to say wouldn't form in her mouth.

"Just spit it out," he said.

"Are you planning to leave me again?" she asked in one long breath.

He looked taken aback and stood up straighter. "I don't know."

Those quietly spoken words weren't the ones she was looking for and they shot dread straight through her.

"It's time for your brother's match," Jay said. "We can talk about this later."

She let him lead her to the volleyball game and, though she pretended to watch, her mind was on his words and the fear in her heart just grew larger.

JAY PULLED THE CAR to a stop in front of Alysse's place. His bike was stored in her garage and he knew he'd be leaving tonight. He had enjoyed hanging out with her, but they both knew she needed something more from him. Something he wasn't going to be able to deliver.

He'd felt the disappointment in her when she'd asked if he was going to leave. He knew he should have just said no, but he didn't want to lie to her.

"You got too much sun today," he said. "Your cheeks are red."

"I always do," she said, the same cold shoulder she'd been giving him all afternoon. "No matter how much sunscreen I use."

"I just get more tanned," he said.

"Have we really come down to banal conversation? You don't have anything more to say to me than that?" she asked, and he heard the anger in her tone. She wanted a fight and he got that, but he wasn't sure he could accommodate her.

"Sorry, just trying to lighten the mood," he said. "I'm not good at this kind of thing. You should know that by now."

"Yeah, you should try harder. You don't encourage anyone to talk to you."

"It's not my scene," he said. "I never know the right thing to say and I always end up feeling like I'm an idiot."

"You are the furthest thing from an idiot that I've ever met."

"That's not what you were thinking earlier," he said.

"True," she said with a laugh. "Do you want to come inside?"

"Yes, but I thought we agreed we'd played this suburban fantasy long enough," he said. He didn't want to have to walk away again but they both knew that... what?

"Let's talk inside. I really don't want to sit out here in the car and have a long conversation."

"Okay," he said. "You go open the windows and I'll get all the stuff from the trunk."

She looked as if she wanted to argue with him, but then she just nodded and got out of the car. He watched her walk up the path to her cute little house and thought how idyllic this place was. The house was comfortable and cozy with a neatly manicured lawn. The neighborhood was friendly but not intrusive. The lady was sexy, sweet and just not right for a man like him.

He cleaned out the car and then walked up to the house. She'd opened all the windows and a nice breeze welcomed him as he stepped inside. He heard the sound of Jimmy Buffett coming from the patio and dumped the cooler in the kitchen before pausing on the threshold between the house and the patio to watch her watering the hibiscus which grew around the edge of her water feature.

A part of him craved this life more than he knew was safe. She'd become an obsession for him and he wanted her. He wanted to say to hell with all the people in her life and just scoop her up and take her away to somewhere special, just the two of them.

But that wasn't ever going to happen.

"Jay?"

"Yes?"

"Do you want a beer?" she asked.

"Nah, I'm good. This place is nice," he said stepping onto the patio and going to sit on one of her Adirondack chairs. She took a seat next to him and then stood up and paced around the garden.

"This isn't really working out, is it?"

"No, it's not. You were right when you said we were playing house, and the last week has been fun though it's not any different from our marriage."

"I know. Do you realize if you spend the night with me tonight it will be the longest we've ever been together?" she asked.

He hadn't realized that. But it explained why he'd been so restless and jittery all day today. "You know you're the only woman I've ever been with for this long."

"That's sad, Jay," she said. "You don't even want to stay longer than a week with me."

"I do," he said. "I'm just not sure how to do this. I want this to be real but for some reason it just isn't."

"I think part of the problem is me," she said. "Earlier when I was talking to Staci I had an epiphany about myself."

"What was it?" he asked when she was quiet.

"I am trying to make you into someone you aren't. I don't think it was a conscious thing, but I was definitely trying to force you to be a part of my group of friends even though I know you prefer being a loner. Even with me you are quiet sometimes and I get that you like that."

He stretched his legs out in front of him. "Why are you doing that?"

"I'm not sure. I don't think it's to punish you but I do think it's some kind of test. Something that I want to prove either to you or me, I'm not sure."

"I guess you still haven't forgiven me," he said.

"I guess not. I thought it would be easy just to ignore the past and somehow use you and get back a little of my own. But that hasn't happened at all. Instead of feeling whole again I just find myself falling deeper and deeper into something that I don't think is ever going to work."

"Me?" he asked.

He knew exactly what she was getting at because he felt the same way. He wanted to be what she needed, but he wasn't about to actually let down his walls and take a chance on getting hurt. He knew she'd been right when she said that he'd purposely left before her in Vegas. That a part of him was always sure if he wasn't the first one out the door he'd be left behind.

And never had that seemed so hard to take than it did right now, looking at Alysse and knowing he wanted her with him for the rest of his life.

11

THE JIMMY BUFFETT CD had switched over to the smooth bluesy tracks of Adele singing about loss in a way that Alysse could relate to at the moment.

The closer she got to Jay the more she felt him slipping away from her. And she was definitely not helping things by trying to force an answer out of him on issues that he'd rather not confront.

At the small pond, she glanced down at the several koi swimming in endless circles. She liked her backyard and felt so comfortable here. She wondered if she would after Jay left. She should never have brought him to the sanctuary that was her home, because now she'd have a hard time not picturing him here.

"Where do we go from here?" she asked at last. She wasn't facing him because she couldn't bear the brutal honesty she saw in his eyes. It would be so much easier if he'd just lie to her a little bit.

"I don't know. I think we have to stop pretending…" he said. "I've been walking on eggshells around you trying not to do anything that will spook you and

apart from that one nightmare I had—I'd say I've suc-
ceeded."

She frowned as she remembered that nightmare and
how scared she'd been for him.

"You have been good about not scaring me," she
agreed. "I've been doing the same thing, sort of, trying to make sure you wouldn't leave me like you did
in Vegas, but to be completely honest, I don't know
what made you leave and hedging my bets isn't helping either one of us."

Hiding and hoping, she admitted it freely now, that
she could maybe be whatever she hadn't been before.
That was scary because she'd really thought she was
over him for good.

"I guess we both need to be just who we really are,"
he said quietly as he walked up next to her. He smelled
of suntan lotion and the sandy beach.

"Yes." Somehow that seemed so much easier to say
than do. She wanted to be free of her fear that he was
leaving her as soon as she let her guard down; however, that wasn't going to happen. "But I don't know
who I am."

Admitting it out loud seemed like the only thing to
do. She pivoted to face him and waited to see his response.

Now she knew why that whirlwind courtship had
worked out so well for her. She hadn't had time to think
or worry about the possibilities. But this time that was
all she'd done. And all that thinking had led her to a
place that made her feel as though she and Jay weren't
going to be able to cobble together the next few days,
much less a lifetime.

Yet she knew she'd grown to know him so much better now than she had before. He was complex. A loner who definitely needed her in his life. A man who would protect everyone around him but would accept no protection himself. A lover who was generous with his body but guarded his heart.

"You do know who you are," he said. "I'm muddling it up by staying here. Let's have breakfast in the morning, I want to spend the day just the two of us—maybe I'll take you on the balloon ride Paulo recommended. No thinking about our jobs or your family. What do you say?" he asked.

She didn't want to. She'd be alone with Jay and that was one thing she still wanted to avoid. "I'm scared."

"Why?" he asked. He glanced down into the koi pond and then put his hands in his back pockets and looked at her. His guarded dark chocolate gaze made her wary. Why couldn't he just trust her?

Why couldn't she just trust him? she asked herself, knowing that if she knew the answers to those questions things would be infinitely better between them.

"It feels as if I'm in one pond and you are in your pond and we just get together for sex. Is that what we're all about?" he asked.

"It's safer," she said. "There is absolutely no danger of me falling for you as long as you stay in your pond and do your own thing."

"I know," he said, taking his hand out of his back pocket and lacing their fingers together. "But neither of us wants a repeat of the last time we got together... do we?"

She looked up at him. The moment of truth. Was

she going to risk her heart on this man again? She'd already seen the proof of what happened when she did.

But if she didn't take this second chance with Jay, would she end up regretting it the rest of her life? Could she live with that?

"No, we don't," she said at last. "I'm willing to try again. Third time's a charm, right?"

"So they say," he said with a wry grin. "I know I wasn't the best when we met up with your friends so maybe we can do it again?"

"Sure. Why don't we invite them over next weekend? We can be the hosts so you'll feel more at ease and we'll have had another entire week to get to know each other. Oh my goodness, a week is hardly any time," she said.

"I'm sorry, I can't offer you more until I know if I'm going to reenlist," he said.

"It's fine. We do better on the fast track," she said. It was as if when she didn't have time to think, she trusted her instincts. She knew that she had something worth fighting for with Jay, but she was afraid to fight for him. Afraid to let him into her heart lest he hurt her again. And no matter how hard she tried to keep from falling for him, she knew she was.

"I don't know how we do better, but I do know that without you by my side…I'm missing something. And I've never had anyone mean that much to me before. I'm a little unsure of how to proceed. I don't want to take a chance on screwing this up," Jay said.

That was probably one of the most honest things he'd ever said to her. She wrapped her broken, fragile heart in those words he'd given her. She was touched by them more than she wanted to be. She understood this man far more now than she had in Vegas. She got that he had demons that she'd never expected and that he needed more from her than she'd been able to offer him.

"Lucien invited me to join him for drinks tomorrow night. Do you want to come along and meet him?" Jay asked.

It was the first time he'd invited her to be a part of his life. He'd gone to her things and talked to her about Sweet Dreams, but he'd never reciprocated much.

"Yes. That sounds nice," she said. "I've been dying to meet some of your friends. I thought maybe you were embarrassed by me."

"I never could be embarrassed by you. You are the best thing that's ever happened to me," he said.

"Really?" she asked. "Don't answer that. I meant to say thank you."

"You're welcome. So how about I pick you up in the morning very early for that balloon ride and then after lunch I will drop you back off…?"

"Okay," she said.

"We can have drinks with Lucien and then I'll take you out. What do you want to do?"

"Anything?"

"Sure," he said. "What's your dream date?"

"Dinner and dancing," she said without hesitating.

"Then that's what we'll do," he said. "I'll be back at six to pick you up."

He walked through her house to the front door and she followed him. She had a reluctant hope that this time maybe things were going to be better for them.

ALYSSE SLEPT RESTLESSLY without Jay by her side, but a part of her knew that she was better off this way. He wasn't ready to make a decision about his career or her. And she needed to be able to protect her heart.

She was awake at five so they could drive up to Temecula. It was very chilly, something she didn't realize until she was on the back of Jay's bike holding on to him. She started shivering and he pulled off on the highway.

"Why are we stopping?" she asked.

"Because you're freezing," he said. He took off his leather jacket and wrapped it around her. He wore a black sweatshirt bearing the Marine Corps emblem under his jacket.

"Will you be warm enough?" she asked.

"I'll be fine as long as you aren't shivering," he said.

"Thank you," she said. "I like your sweatshirt. I notice you don't often wear something with the Corps logo on it. Why is that?"

"People want to buy me coffee and stuff and it makes me uncomfortable," he said.

"They're just saying thanks for doing your job."

"I know that," he said. "But it's a job. The only one I'm trained to do and I'm nothing special."

"Yes, you are," she said.

"You think so?" he asked her.

She could tell he wasn't sure if she was joking around with him and that bothered her.

"Yes, of course I'm sure," she said.

They got back on the bike and finished the drive. There were three other couples waiting to go up in the hot air balloon. Jay had signed them up for a two-hour flight across the valley, and it had sounded fun to her until they climbed in the basket and she saw how fragile the basket was as they started to rise.

"I'm not sure about this," she said.

"What aren't you sure about?" he asked.

"That we won't fall," she said.

"It'd be bad for business if I let you fall," the pilot said with a laugh.

Jay moved to stand behind her, wrapping his arms around her body. He leaned down close to her ear and said, "I've got you and you know I won't let anything happen to you."

She relaxed against him. She might not be sure whether he would stay with her forever, but she knew that he'd protect her with his life. It was still and quiet as they rose up from the valley floor. The sun was just starting to peek over the mountains below. They floated higher and she was almost afraid to speak; the only sound was the occasional hiss of the fire used to inflate the balloon.

"Do you know which vineyard is Paulo's?" Jay asked.

"I don't," she admitted. "I haven't been to visit him and Frida because I'm always so busy at the bakery."

"You work too hard," he said.

"I'm a small-business owner," she said. "If I don't do it, no one else will."

"I don't like that you have to work so hard," he said. "You don't have enough time for yourself."

"That's just the way my life is. You work hard, too," she pointed out.

"But that's different."

"Why? Because you're a man?" she asked.

The pilot chuckled at her tone and Jay tightened his arms around her. "I know better than to answer that question. I just wish that I could pamper you a little bit."

She did like the sound of that. "That'd be nice, but I like my job. If I wasn't working at Sweet Dreams I'd be baking at home and then what would I do with all the baked goods?"

"If I were there I'd eat them," he said.

If he were there. She tried to live for the moment, but she couldn't. She had the feeling he'd already made up his mind to leave. She knew it.

"Time for your champagne brunch," the pilot said, handing them each a glass flute filled with sparkling wine.

Jay took his glass and she took hers. As she stepped out of his arms the gondola rocked a bit, making her reach for him to steady herself. He let her and then arched one eyebrow at her. "What are you doing?"

"I wanted to have a toast," she said.

"Okay," he said.

"To the best ten days we've ever had together," she said at last.

He clinked his glass against hers and took a sip and she did the same. They drank their champagne quickly and Jay pulled her back into his arms. When the pilot told them to look up and smile they did. He handed them a photo a few minutes later; they looked happy, she thought. They looked like a couple who were planning a life together.

Not like two people who could barely manage two

weeks together. She felt sad and didn't enjoy the rest of the ride, but she stayed where she was with Jay's arms around her. She wanted to be able to remember this day and have a nice memory of it.

When they landed, Jay helped her out of the basket and they bought a picture frame from the souvenir shop before getting on his bike and heading back to Oceanside. She was tired and rested her head against his shoulders. She wished there was some way to see into the future, but there wasn't. And when he dropped her off at her house and gave her a quick kiss goodbye, she made herself watch him leave.

She knew he was coming back later to pick her up for their date, but she still wanted to watch him go. Maybe she'd build up an immunity to him leaving so when he finally left for good she wouldn't let him take all of her soul with him.

JAY SENT LUCIEN a text that he was bringing Alysse and the other man had decided he'd bring his girlfriend, too. Drinks turned into dinner and a long, lovely evening. Lucien's girlfriend, India, was tall, almost six feet, and of African descent. She had beautiful skin, close-cut curly hair and the most exotic-looking eyes that Alysse had ever seen.

She felt like a pale plain Jane next to India. It would have been easy to fade into the background except that India wasn't the type of woman who left anyone out. She worked in the fashion industry as a hand model. Honestly, why this woman's face wasn't in front of the camera was beyond Alysse.

Lucien was more guarded, but still, he was relaxed

and he smiled easily whenever India said something that amused him. They were openly affectionate with each other and, in an instant, Alysse realized what she wanted her relationship with Jay to be like. This was how a couple should be, she thought.

Even Jay was a bit more at ease. She'd never say he was relaxed, but instead of being completely silent, he and Lucien had a steady conversation going the entire time they were eating dinner. Occasionally he'd glance over at her.

"How long have you two been together?" India asked after they were seated at a nightclub and the men went to get them drinks.

"It's complicated…we were married for a week and then divorced and now we've been together ten days."

India laughed, a big booming sound that made heads turn. "That *is* complicated. So what's your story? Why are you with Jay?"

No one had ever talked to Alysse that way. "I don't know. He's so different from everyone else in my life and I can't help being attracted to him."

"He is a hottie," India agreed. "But then so is my Lucien."

"You two seem like an interesting couple," Alysse said. Lucien was tall and bald and had a jagged scar running down his forearm. He wore expensive clothing but he still looked rough, as though he'd put a fresh coat of paint over his dents and scratches but she could still see them.

"That's an understatement," India said. "Like you, it was attraction that brought us together first. Then we got to know one another. Underneath all that hotness is a solid man."

"What do you mean by that?"

"Lucien is always there when I need him. I don't even have to say it sometimes and he just shows up," India said. "You know?"

"Yeah, I guess I know what you mean," Alysse said, but she wasn't sure. Jay was still figuring out where he wanted to be.

"You don't," India said, but not unkindly. "Why did you two divorce?"

"He left me," she said. "I know you probably think I'm crazy for trying this again."

"I don't judge another person's heart," India said. "When Lucien and I have our problems, they are monsters and we fight like it's the end of the world, but he's still the man I dream about and I don't think anyone else will do."

"I don't want it to be that way for me," Alysse admitted. "I'm afraid to fall for Jay until he knows what's going on with him. I just want something nice and normal like what you and Lucien have."

"Nothing is nice and normal in love. It's bold and passionate," India said. "Can I give you some advice?"

"Sure," Alysse said.

"Holding back is probably not going to bring you the results you want. Yes, it's safer to try to wait until he knows what he wants but if you aren't being honest with yourself and with him, he's never going to want you. You can't wait for him to be ready for you, you might not still be together if you don't go for it now," India said.

Her words echoed in Alysse's lonely heart. If Jay was her great romance…if they were truly meant to be together, then holding herself back and trying not to love him, well, that wasn't going to help her.

She watched Jay weaving his way through the crowd and she saw his face with its familiar lines of tension and stress. But then he smiled when their gazes met and she understood that she could give him something that he'd never had before. Jay had admitted to being abandoned by his mother. Would the only way he was going to feel safe enough to stay with Alysse be if he felt that she would never leave him?

Her hands literally started sweating and she felt a wave of fear wash over her as her stomach dropped. She didn't know if she could take a huge step like this. She was going to have to put Jay in front of her own dreams of family and happiness and what if this didn't work out? Could she ever trust a man again?

Jay handed her drink to her as Lucien put his and India's drinks on the table.

"Come on, baby. Let's dance," Lucien said, and India slid out of the booth to follow him.

Alysse took a sip of her drink, waiting for Jay to do the same but he was just staring at her.

"Aly, dance with me?" he asked.

"Yes," she said. It seemed as if he was reaching out to her in a way he hadn't before. Today had marked a turning point for both of them. They'd started to let their own guard down. For the first time since she'd woken up alone all those years ago, Alysse felt a tingling near her heart.

"Thank you for today," he said.

"What did I do?" she asked. Not sure where he was headed with this.

"You made me realize how good life can be when you share it with the right woman."

She blushed, knowing her happiness was broadcast on her face.

"You're welcome."

THE LAST OF HIS UNEASINESS from Afghanistan faded away as he pulled Alysse into his arms on the dance floor. The music was upbeat and many couples danced with distance between them, but Jay didn't pay any attention to them. He needed to hold Alysse and to feel that she was still his.

He put his hands on her waist as they swayed together to the music. Lucien had complimented him on being lucky enough to have a woman like Alysse in his life and Jay had been quiet. He had never believed in luck.

No unseen force had ever been looking out for him. He'd managed to get to where he was today by determination and sheer force of will. And as he held this sweet, sexy woman in his arms, he knew that he had to change. It was why he'd thanked her and he could see by her reaction that he'd said the right thing. He had to let her in. Had to enjoy these moments together because he didn't know how long they would last.

He had been searching for some kind of sign. He shook his head and leaned down to kiss her as she glanced up at him. He didn't care that they were in the middle of a crowded dance floor, he only knew that he needed her. He was tired of playing silly games that neither of them could win.

"What was that for?" she asked, leaning up on her tiptoes to speak into his ear.

"Because you make me happy," he said. "No one else ever has."

She hugged him close. "Good. I'm glad."

She pulled back as the rhythm of the music changed and they danced close together, bodies bumping and grinding until Jay thought he was going to explode. He enjoyed the teasing anticipation and could tell that Alysse did as well, because she kept brushing her hands intimately over him.

When it got close to midnight, they said goodbye to Lucien and India and walked hand in hand back to her car. He unlocked her door and then pulled her into his arms, kissing her slowly and seductively.

She held on to him as he tipped her head back and languidly moved his mouth over hers. It was intoxicating. He couldn't get enough of her.

The honking horn of someone driving by pulled them apart; for the first time that he could remember, Jay hadn't been aware of his surroundings.

"Take me home," she said.

He nodded and opened her door for her and helped her get seated. By the time he walked around to the driver's side she had her head tipped back against the seat rest and was staring at him with dreamy eyes.

"You okay?" he asked in his kindest voice.

"Yes. Everything felt right tonight, didn't it?"

He reached over and took her hand, kissing it then putting it on his thigh before he started the car. "Everything was very good tonight."

Her fingers stroked up and down his leg, teasingly dipping to brush against his cock, which was becoming more and more hard with each of her touches.

"India said that I can't hide…"

"What are you hiding from?" he asked, realizing that the fun evening with relaxed company had loosened her tongue.

"You," she admitted. "I don't want to love you again."

His heart stopped. He'd been hoping that she would love him again. That he'd be able to have that sweet attention from her and find somehow that he was worthy of it.

That was what he'd been searching for, he now understood. There was a reason why she didn't want to love him and that was that he'd ruined that emotion for her a long time ago.

No amount of pretending could change his life or rectify the past. He had to face the fact that he needed to leave. That the only solution was to walk away from her.

He glanced over to find her sleepily watching him and he knew that he didn't want to hurt her again. But a part of him was just selfish enough to want to stay. Why should he worry about Alysse and put her needs above his? He didn't know why. He only knew that he did.

She twined their fingers together and leaned her head against his shoulder. They exited the vehicle and she led him to the front door of her cute bungalow. Her perfect normal life and he wasn't strong enough to turn away.

12

ALYSSE DIDN'T WANT to let go of Jay. The night had come alive for her. She'd let her emotions run instead of bottling them up, and she felt almost high from them. God, why hadn't she realized before how good this felt?

As soon as they were in her house she went to him. She'd missed him last night and she was finally able to really admit it. She'd been worried he was going to see her to the door and then leave again.

Having him inside with her made her bold. She knew he was nearing the deadline to decide what he was doing and where he was going and she wanted to make damned sure he knew she wanted him to stay.

"Dance with me here."

"Um, are you sure?" he asked.

She could tell he wanted to retreat and go back to his safe hotel room, but she wasn't going to let him. If Jay left her this time it wasn't going to be without knowing every detail of what he would be missing for the rest of his life.

"Yes. I really liked the way you felt next to me," she

said, leading him into her living room. She hit the light switch and the two side-table lamps came on.

The room was cast in a soft intimate glow and Jay stood in the center. He looked sexy and serious as he waited for her. She smiled at him, a soft sensual expression that he answered.

She went to the iPod dock that she kept in her living room hooked up to speakers. She had always liked music and hadn't scrimped on the sound system when she'd purchased it. Now she was glad because she wanted every detail of this night to be perfect. It was the only way she was going to be able to convince him to stay.

She flipped through her playlists and found what she was looking for. The song she wanted to dance with him to had been playing in the lounge the first night they'd gone for a drink in Vegas. She only listened to it when she was feeling nostalgic and a bit melancholy, but she wanted that to change. She wanted to reclaim the song as she felt she'd reclaimed the man.

As Michael Bublé crooned the tune "For Once In My Life," she moved slowly toward Jay.

"It's our song," he said.

"Yes," she agreed. "I didn't think you would remember."

"I remember every detail of that week with you. I can't have a steak without remembering eating a bite off the end of your fork. Or taste a strawberry without remembering the way you crushed them on your breast and invited me to lick them off."

She shivered remembering how free she'd felt with him back then because she'd trusted him completely.

"I haven't been that daring in a long time," she admitted.

"That's my fault," he said.

He held his hand out to her and met her halfway, pulling her into his arms and swaying gently with the song. His hands moved up and down her back.

"Do you remember our wedding?" she asked.

"I do," he admitted. "You wore the simplest white sheath dress that had a deep V in the front like this."

He drew his finger along her collarbone and then pulled the fabric of her neckline down until it was between her breasts.

"The slopes of your breasts were visible and as soon as you walked into the chapel it was all I could look at."

"Really?"

"Yes. I wanted to do this," he said, lowering his head and dropping very soft kisses against the globes of her breasts. "But then I looked up at your neck and saw the line of your jaw and that mouth of yours. You have the most luscious mouth. All I can think about when we are together is kissing you."

"Then do it," she said.

He leaned in and rubbed his lips over hers. She sighed and felt the magic of the evening deepening for her.

"What do you remember? First impressions of me in the chapel?" he asked.

"When I stepped inside and saw you waiting for me I couldn't breathe. You looked so handsome in your dress uniform. I didn't realize how good-looking you were until that moment. You stood so straight and at attention and then our eyes met and I felt a thrill all the way to my toes. I thought you were mine."

"I was."

But then he'd left. And she'd convinced herself that a feeling that strong could have been one-sided.

She wrapped her arms around his lean waist and rested her head on his chest. He put one hand on the back of her head and rubbed his palm over her back. Keeping her close. The song played on and they swayed together to the music.

It was a quick song, and when it ended she flushed as Marvin Gaye's "Let's Get It On" was the next song to start playing.

He chuckled. "We never danced to this one before."

"I know. It's not exactly the subtlety I was trying for."

"Hell, this is my kind of song," he said. Putting his hands on her hips and grinding against her. She did the same, moving her hands up and down his chest slowly loosing buttons until his shirt was open and she could touch his hard muscles.

"I love your chest," she said, pushing his shirt off his shoulders. His shoulders were broad and strong, his skin warm to her touch.

He let her have her way with him, caressing him however she wanted. She traced his spine and then let her fingers dip into his pants to caress the dusting of hair at the small of his back. He groaned. She slowly came around to his front trailing her fingers along that edge between bare flesh and cloth. Then she used her grip on his waistband to draw him closer to her. She tipped her head back and put her free hand around his neck and drew his head down to hers.

"I love the feel of your hands on my body. No one has ever touched me the way you do, Aly."

"Good," she said. She wanted to brand him all over so that he'd never forget her or these nights they'd spent together. He'd marked her deep in her soul a long time ago and she was just realizing that was why no other man could satisfy her the way he did.

His breath brushed over her lips first and then she took his mouth. His hands went to her back, drawing her as close as possible to his body until they were intimately pressed together. Their kisses were long and languid as they swayed to the music, not even noticing when it stopped playing.

The hand at her waist slowly gathered the fabric of her skirt and drew it up the back of her legs until she felt one of his big warm hands on her buttocks. She gyrated against him and felt him cupping her and pulling her closer to his rock-hard erection. She moaned as the tip of his cock hit her in just the right place.

She used the hand she had at his waistband to unbutton his pants, but didn't undo the zipper at first. Just teased him by resting a hand there. She felt his cock jump against her fingers as she stroked him before she lowered the zipper enough to slide her hand into the front of his pants.

He was so incredibly hard. She stroked the tip of his cock before letting her fingers drift lower to ride along the side of his shaft. She wished this moment with Jay would never end. She felt so alive, yet so in control.

With both hands she pushed his pants and boxers to the floor and he stepped out of them.

He was completely naked. She moved back to admire Jay. She understood that passion was the key to being truly free. Wasn't that what she'd discovered sitting in the club? And she felt passion as she looked at her man with his muscled chest and the light dusting of hair leading to his manhood, which stood proud and erect because of her.

She felt a surge of love and lust for him. She'd been completely crazy if she'd ever thought it could be just sex between her and Jay and then she'd move on. He was the only man she'd been unable to banish from her thoughts and dreams.

She walked over to him and he simply stood there. She took his hand and led him to the leather couch a few feet away. She pushed him back on the couch and he sank down with all the masculine grace she'd come to expect from him.

She went to kneel next to him on the couch but he stopped her. "Take your panties off."

Her pulse raced and she felt her pussy moisten at his words. Slowly, she lifted the hem of her dress to reveal first her thighs and then the edge of her panties. As she reached underneath, she slowly drew the tiny lace underwear down her legs.

She stood still, with her skirt held in one hand and turned so that she gave him a full view and bent low to pick up the scrap of cloth. She glanced over her shoulder at him and saw that he was staring at her butt. She tossed her panties on the ground at his feet and then moved back to his side.

He put his hands underneath her skirt, running his fingernails up and down the length of her thighs until she was panting in his grasp. He teased her by coming close to her intimate flesh but never touching it. She reached for his cock, caressing his entire shaft and then lowering her head to lick the tip of it before taking him into her mouth.

His hips jerked from the couch as she cupped him and continued to work his shaft with her mouth. He moved her body around until he could reach her clit with his fingers. She felt him separating her inner lips and then the light brush of his finger against her throbbing core. Moisture pooled between her legs and she felt his forefinger slip lower until he entered her. She moaned against his cock as he excited her, pushing her to the brink.

She sucked more strongly on his cock and tasted a salty drop of him and she swallowed it. But then he pulled her away.

"I don't want it to be like this when I come," he said, his voice rough and low. His skin was flushed and she was aroused to the point where she didn't know anything except desire.

"Come inside me, Jay. I feel so empty without you."

"Are you ready for me?" he asked, touching her between her legs again. All she could do was nod frantically, waiting for him to finish what they'd started.

"That's not ready enough," he said. "Unzip your dress."

She reached for the side zipper and undid it. The fabric gaped away from her body but still covered her.

She ignored it as she tried to climb on his lap, needing his cock inside her now.

He stopped her with his hands on her waist. "Take your dress off."

"Jay, we don't need to draw this out. I want you inside me now."

"No," he told her, his tone serious. "I want to take my time with you tonight, Aly. Do what I said."

His firm voice excited her that much more and she frantically ripped at her own clothing trying to get the dress off. Her arms got tangled in it and Jay helped her free herself. She was naked except for the lacy demi-bra she wore.

"Straddle me."

She did as he ordered, climbing on his lap. He lowered his head and kissed the full globes of her breasts, which were bared by the demi-bra. His hands slid down her back to her buttocks and he drew her forward so that she rode the edge of his cock.

Her grip on his shoulders tightened and she tried to shift around to bring the top of his erection to her opening and get him inside her, but he wasn't going to be rushed.

One of his hands slid up her back and unfastened her bra. The straps loosened and he used his teeth to pull the fabric away from her breasts. She felt the tip of his tongue on her areole, stroking it until her nipple tightened. Then she felt the warmth of his mouth on her nipple as he sucked on it.

She reached between them and took his cock in her hand and positioned him exactly where she needed him. She thrust herself onto his cock, driving him deep to the heart of her. She rocked her hips back and forth while he continued to suckle her.

He tore his mouth from her breast and looked up at her through half-closed eyes. His hands came to her hips and he began to thrust harder and quicker. She lost control of their embrace as he tilted her head toward his and slipped his tongue teasingly into her mouth as he came inside her.

She shuddered as her own orgasm overtook her. She kept on riding him to prolong her orgasm and then collapsed against him. She relaxed, tracing the lines of his pectorals and drawing a heart over it. She closed her eyes trying not to let her emotions get the better of her, but she knew the truth as soon as he looked her in the eye.

She loved him.

She wanted to say it but knew better than to say anything. She was still too afraid to trust herself or him.

India's words came back to haunt her. Where was the passion that she was using to embrace life? How was Jay ever going to know that she needed him to stay until she told him?

"Jay?"

"Shh...don't talk," he said. He lifted her, stood and walked down the short hall to her bedroom. He set her on her feet in the doorway of the bathroom, and she watched as he went to her garden tub and slowly turned on the taps.

"But I think there is something I need to say."

"I'm sure there is, but there is something magical going on between us right now and I don't want it to end. I want this one night, Aly. Is that okay?" he asked.

She nodded. She wanted it, too. She wanted to pretend that this was a world she'd never been in before. That all of her dreams were coming true with this man. She gathered candles from under the sink as he filled the tub with water and her rose-scented bubble bath. She lit the candles and set them on the edge of the tub.

Jay lifted her into water that was the perfect temperature and then climbed into the tub and sat down behind her. She lowered herself gently into the water and settled back against him. His arms were around her and she rested her head once again on his chest. She felt his big arms around her and knew that falling in love with Jay hadn't made any of her problems disappear. He was still a man at a crossroads, and who knew what path he was going to choose? But for tonight she didn't regret falling for him.

He had mended her broken heart and given her back some of the romantic dreams he'd stolen from her. He slowly bathed her and she felt tears sting the backs of her eyes as he treated her so tenderly. Jay was a rough man through the life he'd lived but tonight with her he was as gentle as any man could be and he'd found his way right back into her heart.

JAY DIDN'T ALLOW HIMSELF to think beyond this night. He'd had a few experiences in his life that he kept protected in his memory. Most of them involved this woman and he didn't want anything—not even himself—to mar this night.

She was special to him. More so than he'd realized when he'd come back to San Diego looking for answers. Now he had those answers and he knew without a shadow of a doubt that Alysse was the only woman in the world that he wanted to spend the rest of his life with.

And if life were as easy as television shows and Hollywood movies made it seem, that would be all it would take for them to commit themselves and spend the rest of their days together. But this wasn't a TV show or movie and he knew that despite his good intentions he'd never be the man that Alysse needed.

She knew it, he suspected, but because they'd spent so much time with each other she was probably thinking, as he was, that there was some way to make the magic last for them. But the truth was there was no elixir that would cure him of his past. No potion that would make his shattered soul whole and no real chance that he'd be able to live in this cute little suburban house with Alysse for the rest of his days.

The water was starting to cool, so he stood up and climbed from the tub, drying himself off quickly before helping Alysse. He dried her carefully from head to toe, lingering over her entire body because he'd never have enough of touching her. He dreamed of her skin and the softness of it when they were apart.

"Why are you treating me like I'm made of glass?" she asked.

He wasn't sure what to say. Didn't know what was the right or wrong thing and looking into her amazing blue eyes he settled for the truth. "To me you are the most precious thing."

She swallowed hard and then threw herself into his arms and he held her close, breathing in the floral scent of her skin. He closed his eyes and tried to figure out a way he could keep Alysse without shattering her dreams for the future.

But he'd seen the way she'd looked at Lucien and India tonight. He knew she wanted a relationship like that and he couldn't give that to her. He just wasn't that kind of man.

He found her nightshirt on the hook behind the bathroom door and put it on her before leading her to her bed. Once they were both settled beneath the covers and she was nestled close against his side, cuddled up on his chest, he felt her relax. She put her hand over his chest and kissed him right there over his heart.

"Thank you," she said.

"For?" he asked. He didn't think he'd done anything for her that she didn't deserve. Alysse had given him gifts that he'd just taken blindly before he recognized how much she meant to him.

"The best day," she said. "I have spent the entire day with you and it wasn't at all what I expected."

"It wasn't?"

"No. You were everything I ever dreamed you would be. I thought this morning that we were headed for a breakup tonight but the day turned around, didn't it?"

Her words were like a dagger to him. He couldn't give her days like this. Today had almost been the end of him because he'd felt too much. Men who had this much to lose never made it back.

"Today was nice," he said. "But it wasn't anything too special."

"It was to me. No one—not even my dad—has ever given me a day like this. You made me feel like a princess and not the little-girl kind."

"What kind then?" he asked her.

"Like a woman who can have it all. You were my white knight today. It was perfect."

She was killing him. She was unable to contain her excitement, and he knew that was because she'd started caring for him again.

And he didn't want to—hell, he wasn't going to let her down again. So if that meant that he had to stay here with her for the rest of his life then he'd do it. He didn't know how he'd do it but he'd figure it out.

For that smile he'd move the world.

"Why are you watching me like that?"

"Like what?" he asked.

"Kind of sad and sort of…scared almost," she said.

"Don't worry about it," he said. "And I don't know about being any knight. My armor is tarnished. Can't you see that? There is nothing hero-like about me at all."

She gently kissed him on the chest. "Everything about you is heroic."

He knew she was wrong. Still, he stayed where he was and held her as she drifted off to sleep. He was surrounded by Alysse and it was the closest thing to heaven that he knew he'd ever experience in this life or the next one.

Her breath stirred the hair on his chest and, as her sleep deepened, she snored softly and even that tiny imperfection just made him love her more. He held her as close as he dared so he wouldn't disturb her, and he felt the way he had back in that Vegas hotel room—afraid of her and for her. Afraid to be the man she clearly needed him to be because he wasn't sure he really had it in him.

He'd never in his life wanted anything more than he wanted to keep Alysse with him. But he knew just as surely as the desire formed inside him that he would hurt her, and he couldn't live with himself if he did that.

He tried different scenarios in his head, trying to figure out how he was going to be able to keep her safe and keep her in his arms at the same time, but there wasn't one that would keep her happy.

As the first fingers of dawn crept across the room he loosened himself from her hold and slid out of her bed. He found his clothing in the living room and dressed quickly, getting a hard-on from remembering the sexy dance they'd shared here last night.

And from the memories of their wedding night. He picked up his leather jacket, which she'd kept from the morning balloon ride, and the picture of the two of them that the pilot had taken fell out. He stooped to pick it up and then stood staring at them. He looked too hard for her.

She deserved that white knight she'd always wanted. A man who could love her and not worry about her leaving. A man she didn't have to worry would leave her. And if he didn't walk out this door today, Jay knew there was always a chance that he'd be taken from her life by war.

He had no other training and even if he worked with Lucien there was no guarantee that he'd be back home with Alysse every night. He'd promised her mother that if he couldn't ensure Alysse would be happy with him, he'd get out of her life and never come back.

At the time he'd hoped to find a way to stay with her but now it seemed there wasn't a way. And he knew exactly what he needed to do. But it was harder this time.

Last time it had only been lust between them and this time he had started caring for her, and that made each step he took heavy and hard.

He walked to the door that overlooked her backyard and remembered standing there with her at the pond and feeling maybe a little hope for the future. But he'd been kidding himself since the moment he'd returned here.

He was truly a loner and he only knew how to be comfortable in his own skin when he was on a mission in the field with his scout next to him. He liked the world through the view of his scope. It was safer that way. He could control everything when he was looking through the sight.

He knew that his life would always be gray after this, but it was better than attempting to be someone he wasn't and failing miserably. Better than trying to make things work with Alysse and breaking her heart again, only worse because he'd seen the real woman this time, not the girl on vacation. He slowly turned and looked around her living room before walking through it toward the door.

He had hoped to find answers here and he guessed that he had. He'd hoped that maybe this time he could make their ending different. He knew he was the one who was leaving, but he also knew it was just a matter of time before Alysse knew that he couldn't be the man she wanted him to be.

He'd got to the foyer when he heard the creak of the

bedsprings and knew he could either run out the front door as he had before or wait and confront her. And he wished he were a stronger man, but he reached for the front door, undoing the deadbolt and turning the handle as quietly as he could.

"Running again?"

13

ALYSSE HAD GOTTEN USED TO sleeping with Jay and sleeping lightly enough that when he got out of bed he'd waken her. She'd thought at first that maybe he was just getting a drink of water as he sometimes did, but then, as the time lengthened, she knew he was leaving.

She'd lain there in her bed debating confronting him and suddenly it seemed so cowardly for her to be lying there while he was sneaking out. So she'd gone to confront him and found him standing at the front door with his hand on the handle and her heart broke.

He wasn't leaving for work or an early meeting, he was leaving for good and they both knew it.

"I'm sorry," he said.

"Don't be. Just tell me why," she said.

"I think I'm going back into the Corps," he said.

As if that would explain everything and make this all okay somehow. "Really? Why did you stay last night then? What was that all about?"

She was beyond upset and well into angry now and she wasn't about to take this sitting down. He was leaving her twice. This was her worst nightmare and here it was coming true. Dammit, she had been planning to be the stronger one this time, why wasn't she?

"Can we not do this?" he asked. There was something in his expression that she couldn't read and that bothered her more than she wanted to admit.

"No, we're doing this," she said. "The last time I just let you walk out on me. Well, to be honest, I didn't hear you leave, but even if I had I would have lain there and let you go without a fight. But I'm not willing to do that this time."

He sighed. It was a heavy one as he finally came toward her. He stopped when there was six inches between them but it might as well have been a gap as big as the Grand Canyon. He was eons away from her and there was nothing she was going to say that would bring him back.

But last night she'd admitted she loved him. Last night he'd been the tender man she'd always dreamed of finding and she wasn't going to let him throw that all aside. She just didn't know what she could do to make him stay.

"Leaving isn't easy for me," he said. "But I can't stay. I saw your face last night when we were in the club with Lucien and India. I know that you hope that someday we will be that kind of a couple. But I can't be like that. I'm always going to be more inward and less social."

She shook her head. "I never asked you to change."

"I know that. You won't do it either. But I'd have to watch you wither and grow disappointed in me because I'm not the man you need me to be."

She wondered if that were true. But then she realized

that even if there were shards of honesty in that state-ment, the reason he was leaving was more complex. "I don't believe that's why you're sneaking out of here, Jay Michener. You're leaving because you're afraid you will like it here. That you'll start enjoying the life that we could have together. And you're afraid. Afraid to change and let yourself really feel something."

"And you're afraid to just let me go," he said. "As much as I enjoy being alone, you're afraid of that very thing. You surround yourself every hour of the day with family and friends, and you have to ask yourself why? What is it you are so afraid of?"

"I don't see that," she said. "You're grasping at straws because if you aren't looking at a target through the safety of your scope then you don't let yourself relax. You aren't living life. You are observing it."

He looked taken aback. And she felt a twinge of guilt at what she'd said, but there was no hiding from this. He was leaving and there was nothing she could say that would make him stay.

"You may be right," he said, a sudden quietness in him and in his voice. "But I don't think I can change. I'm sorry, Aly. I wanted a different ending for us. But I think I was fooling myself into believing I was a dif-ferent sort of man."

She closed the gap between them and reached out to touch his beard-stubbled jaw. "You don't have to be a different man, you just have to be the man you are inside here."

She drew her hand down his chest and tapped lightly over his heart. She knew that as tough as he was on the outside, Jay was soft inside. And that was why he fought so hard not to let anyone in, even her.

She hugged him because she was going to miss him more than he could ever know. His arms stayed by his sides and she felt her heart break wide open. It wasn't his fault that he couldn't love her and there was nothing she could have done to make herself not love him. She'd thought she could bring her warrior in from battle and show him the beauty of being a part of her community, but he wasn't ready to give up fighting and she doubted he ever would be.

"Goodbye."

He stepped back and looked at her and she easily read the anguish in his eyes.

"I didn't mean to hurt you again," he said.

It bothered her more than she wanted to admit that he knew that he'd hurt her but somehow hadn't been able to see that she loved him.

"Is that really your only regret?" she asked.

"No, but we don't have time for me to list them all," he said, turning and walking toward the door.

"Coward," she said. "There's no pride in walking away now. You are just proving that you aren't all you can be."

"That's the army slogan," he said.

"I don't care whose it is. You pride yourself on being a soldier, a warrior, but you don't have the guts to stay and fight for something you said you wanted. Or have you changed your mind?"

JAY HADN'T EXPECTED Alysse to let him just walk out the door but he didn't expect this amount of anger. Why not? Was he that insensitive that he'd missed something important here? He knew that she'd been hoping—hell, he knew nothing. She was still a big mystery to him and it seemed as if she always would be.

"I'm not a coward. I'm doing this for you," he said.

"For me?" she asked, the incredulity in her voice enough to make him take a step back toward her.

"Yes, for you. Do you think I like knowing that even though you are with me I'm not the man you want? Do you think I like seeing disappointment in your eyes?"

"No. I never meant for you to feel that way," she said. "I can work on that."

She could try, but it wouldn't change the fact that he was always going to be who he was inside and she couldn't change that or accept it. He needed to make this break and never come back here again. He needed to walk away and keep Alysse tucked safely into his memories.

"You can't. We've been trying to build something out of nothing here. That's my fault. I'm sorry this didn't work out better."

"Sure," she said. "I guess it doesn't matter if I love you."

His heart stopped beating for a second. No one in his adult life had uttered those words to him and he wanted to hold them close and hold her close. Was there a way he could make this work? Could he be the man she needed him to be?

He'd thought about the job with Lucien but to be honest he was afraid to risk it and find that he couldn't stomach the job. He was a mess and had not been in the right place to start up his relationship with Alysse again. He'd made a mistake but he couldn't bring himself to say those words out loud.

She watched him carefully, he suspected she was looking for some kind of sign that he'd figure out how to work this through, but he was tired of keeping them both on this roller coaster. He just wasn't the right kind of man for the long haul. It didn't matter that he felt like he should want something more. He was too afraid to go after what it was he wanted. He deserved the moniker of coward that she'd given him.

"Your love is a gift I will treasure forever," he said.

She shook her head. "No, you won't. You'll shove it deep down inside you so you don't have to deal with it. I'm just sorry that I couldn't show you that life is more than your missions."

But she had. And that was the part that scared him. He stalked back over to her, putting his hands on her shoulders. "Of course I saw that. Do you think I don't crave this idyllic life with every fiber of my being?"

"Then why are you leaving?"

"Because I know how quickly this can be taken away. You know who makes the biggest sacrifices in Afghanistan?"

She shook her head.

"Those with the most to lose. Those with spouses and kids back home. It's never the loners. And I've been shown a lot of karma in this life. Who's to say if I try to make this work that we will have a lifetime together?"

"No one can guarantee that. No one," she said.

She lifted her hand toward him, brushing her fingers over his brow. Then down the side of his face.

"I'm willing to take the chance, Jay."

He knew he could make this easy on himself. Just open his arms and draw her into them. Pretend for her sake that everything would be okay. But he couldn't do it. He didn't want to cause her more pain by staying. And a part of him was sure he would. Or worse—he'd stay and she'd realize that the love she thought she had for him wasn't real. He didn't want to leave her. Hell, he wasn't an idiot. It was just that he knew that by going now he'd save them a much bigger heartbreak later.

"I'm not willing to."

Her arms dropped to her sides. She stared into his eyes with that electric-blue gaze of hers and he felt that she was peering deep into his soul. He hoped that she didn't really see into that bottomless well because he'd seen too much in this lifetime. Things he never wanted her to know about. She sighed and then nodded.

"Okay, then."

She walked around him to the front door and opened it. The sun was coming up over the horizon and the neighbors were out walking their dogs and getting ready for work. A perfect normal morning and yet he felt shell-shocked. As if he'd just withstood a barrage of enemy fire.

He wanted to pat down his body and look for holes but he knew exactly where the pain was coming from. He crossed the small hallway of her house and when he got to the threshold he knew that if he took one more step he'd never be welcomed back here again.

He was afraid of that step and hesitated. If he thought there was a way that he could have her and keep her for the rest of his life he wouldn't do this but he couldn't see it.

"Have a good life, Jay," she said. "I hope you find some peace."

He nodded, and as soon as he was outside on her front porch he heard the door close behind him with a finality that echoed down to his boots.

THREE DAYS LATER Jay went to the enlistment office on base to sign his papers, but the entire time his heart felt heavy and Alysse's words kept ringing in his ears. Was he afraid to change?

The weather didn't seem to notice his mood and stayed sunny and temperate as if to shame him with his own black thoughts. He missed Alysse more than he'd thought he would. He hadn't had a single night's sleep since he'd left her because he kept waking up to search for her.

Hell, he knew that was partly why he was right back here. This was the one place in the world that he trusted. Then he admitted that wasn't true anymore. He trusted himself when he was with Alysse and he should never have left her.

In fact, he loved her. He'd been in love with her for the last four years. He'd struggled to keep his distance from her only because he'd never felt good enough for her. He still wasn't sure that he was good enough for her, but the way she'd fought with him had told him that he was the man she wanted.

But leaving the way he had… Trying to sneak out on her again. He hoped he hadn't killed her love for him. It was going to be impossible to win her back.

He knew he could do it because she loved him, but he had to plan it. And do a better job than he had when he'd called her to the beach at the Hotel Del Coronado.

The first thing he did was to sign his separation papers for the Marines. Then he left Pendleton and headed toward the offices of Company B. Someone who worked as hard as Alysse deserved a man—a husband who worked just as hard, if not harder.

He pulled into the parking lot and felt a moment of sheer terror as he realized he'd left the only home he'd had since turning eighteen. To be honest, he hadn't had a home since his mother had left when he was eight. His dad had never been good with people, a trait Jay guessed had been passed on to him. But he was damned sure he was going to be good with Alysse. And he'd do everything in his power to make sure they were never apart again.

"You okay, Jay?" Lucien asked, coming out of the offices of Company B and standing next to Jay on his bike.

"No. I'm not. I just left the Corps." Oh, man. He was unsure of this decision as soon as he said the words out loud, but then he thought of going home to Alysse every night and some of the tension eased.

"Is that a good thing or a bad thing?" Lucien asked.

"It's going to be a very good thing if I can convince you to give me a job," Jay said.

"It's yours, buddy. I wanted you to work with me from the beginning," Lucien said. "Come inside and we can get the contract drawn up and have you sign it."

Jay got off his bike and followed Lucien inside.

"So what made you decide it was time to go private-sector?" Lucien asked him.

"Alysse," Jay said. He wasn't ever going to be comfortable talking about his personal life, but in this instance he didn't mind sharing it with Lucien. "I want to marry her again and do everything right this time."

"Good for you. Got an idea of how to propose?"

"No," Jay said. "And I screwed up so I have to win her back."

"Can I help?" Lucien asked.

"Be my best man?"

"I will."

It took forty-five minutes to get the contract drawn up and for Jay to sign all the paperwork that was needed. When he left the Company B offices he was an official employee.

Next on his list was a call to Toby. He needed Alysse's family on his side if he had any chance of pulling off his plan. He knew he'd never be able to trick her to the beach twice, and it was very important to him that he have all the details right this time. He wanted her to know how much she meant to him.

"Hello, this is Dresden."

"Toby? This is Jay Michener."

There was silence on the other end of the phone.

"Is Alysse all right?"

She hadn't told her family that he'd walked out on her again. He felt shocked and surprised. "Yes. I mean I think so. I messed up and I need your help to get her back."

"You need my help? What the hell did you do now?"

"Ran away again. But your sister held her own with me, which I'm sure isn't any surprise to you."

"No, it's not. Alysse knows how to give as good as she gets and she is brutally honest sometimes."

"She called me a coward," Jay admitted.

"Damn. You must have really upset her," Toby said.

"I did, but I want her back, Toby. Will you help me?" Jay asked.

There was a long silence on the other end of the phone. "If I help you it's because I love my sister and I know that she wants you in her life."

"Thank you, Toby. I want to be worthy of being in her life."

"What's your plan?" Toby asked.

He outlined what he had in mind and after a few minutes Toby agreed to assist him. "If she says no, that's it. I want you out of here for good."

"If she says no then I don't deserve her."

Jay drove back to the Hotel Del Coronado where Toby met him in the lobby. They spent the afternoon seeing to every detail and when the evening rolled around Jay got dressed in a tuxedo he'd purchased from Nordstrom's with Candi's help earlier in the day. He stared at himself hard in the mirror and he hoped that whatever Alysse had seen in him when he was in his dress blues, she'd see in him tonight.

He'd never needed another person as much as he needed her and it would be damned hard for him not to worry. He'd never depended on another person as much as he did on Alysse. And he had no idea how she'd react tonight.

14

"SWEET DREAMS BAKERY, home of the incredible red velvet dream cupcakes," Alysse spoke into the phone. It had been the longest three days of her life and now that it was almost closing time on Friday afternoon she wanted to get out of the bakery and go back to her home and hide away.

But she couldn't do that because her home was now filled with memories of Jay. She couldn't believe he'd left her once again. Worse, that she was still in love with him.

"Hello," the caller said. His voice was very familiar.

"Toby?"

"Yes. I have a dessert emergency," he said.

"An emergency?" she asked. "What kind of emergency?"

"It's Molly's parents' anniversary and I told her I'd order a replica wedding cake and deliver it to the Hotel Del Coronado tonight by six."

"Toby! I can't make a replica wedding cake in four hours," she said.

"It doesn't have to be huge or perfect or anything like that. I just need something. Maybe two layers."

"Two layers. I don't know. I have some cakes that I baked for a wedding tomorrow that I could use. If you want me to do this, you have to come down here with a photo so I can decorate it properly."

"Fine, but then I need you to deliver it because I have to get back to their party, which you are invited to, as well. Dress fancy."

Her brother was a lunatic. "I am supposed to bake a cake, haul it across town for Molly's parents and get dressed up, too?"

"Yeah. Is there a problem? Mom said she'd drop off your dress."

"Isn't that great. Anything else?"

"Nope, that's all. Will you bring Jay with you?" he asked.

She bit her lower lip. "I think he's busy tonight. So it'll just be me."

"I was wrong about him," Toby said. "I'm glad you gave him a second chance."

She wasn't. Hell, that was a lie, of course she was glad she'd given him a second chance. The last two weeks of her life more than made up for the previous four years of being alone. The only bad part was that they weren't together still.

"Don't forget the photo."

"I'm emailing it to you. Check your phone," Toby said. "Thanks, sis, you're a lifesaver."

"Yeah, right. Love ya."

"Ditto," Toby said, finishing the call.

She opened the attachment on the email from Toby

and was taken aback by the cake they'd selected. It matched the one from her wedding to Jay in Vegas. There was no way anyone in her family could know that because they hadn't attended the ceremony or even seen the cake, but it made her tear up as she looked at it.

She put two more cakes in the oven to replace the ones she was using for Molly's parents. And then got to work decorating a cake that made her heart break.

She finished the anniversary cake just as her mom came through the back door with a garment bag over one shoulder. Alysse was alone in the shop because Staci had gone to L.A. to do some more prep work for her audition on *Premiere Chef.*

"Hello, honey," her mom said, coming over and giving her a kiss.

She kissed her mom hello then shooed her hand out of the frosting bowl as Candi swiped her finger through it. "You look nice."

"Thanks. Toby is in the hot seat tonight," her mom said. "Molly just found out about this last-minute stuff with you. She was not pleased."

"He should have said that he asked me to do it a while ago," Alysse said.

"He couldn't lie to her. Would you lie to Jay?" her mom asked.

"No," she admitted. But apparently she had no problem lying to the rest of her family. She hated that she hadn't told her mom or brother that she and Jay weren't together anymore, but she was so afraid of looking stupid.

She put the cake in the van while her mom tidied up the kitchen. Then she got dressed in a pale yellow dress that she knew hadn't come from her closet. Her mom loved buying her things and, to be honest, Alysse didn't mind.

"Okay, I'm ready to go."

"You look beautiful, sweetie."

"Thanks, Mom."

When they arrived at the hotel Toby was waiting in the lobby. "I need Mom to come with me. Will you take the cake down to the beach?"

"Sure," she said. "I need a valet cart though. It's kind of big."

"No problem," Toby said. He took care of getting her a cart and helped her with the cake. Then he hugged her close.

"What was that for?"

"Just because I love you," he said.

"Love you, too, Tobe. But if you make me do this again I'm going to strangle you."

"I will never ask you to do this again," he promised.

As she followed the path to the beach she couldn't help but remember the last time she'd been here, supposedly trying to rekindle a romance and instead finding Jay waiting for her.

She wished that would happen again. But she knew that she would have better luck wishing for snow right now than Jay being here with her.

She got close and saw that the beach was set up for a dinner party with tables and chairs and in the middle a dance floor with a table nearby that she assumed was for the cake. A man stood there with his back toward her. He wore a formal jacket and there was something distinctive about the breadth of his shoulders.

She stopped abruptly and stared. "Jay?"

He turned around and a cascade of emotions ran through her. "What are you doing here?"

"Waiting for you," he said.

"Waiting for me?"

"Yes. I set this up. I wanted to do things right this time."

"I'm not entirely sure what you mean," she said.

He came to her and took her hand, leading her to the middle of the dance floor.

"I was a coward for leaving again. Even as I walked out of your door I knew I loved you, but I was so afraid to stay. Afraid I couldn't be the man you needed me to be," he said.

"What changed your mind?"

"You did," he said. "You have haunted me every single second since I left you. And I know now that I need you with me, Aly. I don't want to be alone anymore."

"But—"

"I know I haven't given you much to believe in, but I want you to know that I am changing. I quit the Corps and got a job with Company B. I confessed to your mom and Toby that I'd hurt you again."

"Oh, I hadn't mentioned that to them," she said.

"I think you did that because you knew I wasn't leaving for good this time," he said. "You took a big chance on letting me go and had to hope that I loved you enough to come back this time. And I do. I love you."

She blinked at the tears that were stinging her eyes and looked up at him. "Are you sure?"

"Yes. Very sure. Do you think I can redeem myself and be your hero again?"

"Yes," she said. "I love you, Jay Michener. If you ever try to leave me again I might have to hurt you."

"I never will," he promised. "In fact, I want to do something…will you wait here a minute?"

"Yes," she said.

While Jay strode up the path she moved the cake onto the table so it was out of harm's way. Eventually, hotel staff showed up to man the deejay booth and then her family and friends arrived. They all sat down at the tables and Jay came back to her in the center of the dance floor and got down on one knee.

"Alysse Dresden, in front of all of our family and friends, will you marry me and be the light in my life?"

"I will," she said.

Jay smiled up at her and pulled a small ring box from his pocket. Taking out the diamond ring, he slipped it on her finger and stood up to kiss her.

As he embraced her she knew she'd found something more than she'd ever expected. By taking that rush order for a redemption cupcake, she'd found the happiness she'd been missing. The man who was the other half of her soul.

* * * * *

The World of Mills & Boon®

There's a Mills & Boon® series that's perfect for you. We publish ten series and, with new titles every month, you never have to wait long for your favourite to come along.

Blaze®

Scorching hot, sexy reads
4 new stories every month

By Request

Relive the romance with the best of the best
9 new stories every month

Cherish™

Romance to melt the heart every time
12 new stories every month

Desire™

Passionate and dramatic love stories
8 new stories every month

Have Your Say

You've just finished your book. So what did you think?

We'd love to hear your thoughts on our
'Have your say' online panel
www.millsandboon.co.uk/haveyoursay

- Easy to use
- Short questionnaire
- Chance to win Mills & Boon® goodies